Praise for *Calling for a Blanket Dance*

WINNER OF THE PEN/HEMINGWAY AWARD
Finalist for the *LA Times* Art Seidenbaum Award for First Fiction •
Finalist for the Aspen Words Literary Prize • One of *Booklist*'s
Top First Novels for 2022 • A *Kirkus Reviews* Best Book of 2022 •
Longlisted for the 2023 Carnegie Medal for Excellence in Fiction

"With intricate prose and unflinching vernacular, Oscar Hokeah chronicles a family and a community . . . We need these characters and their testimonies. But more than that, we crave—I crave—this kind of honest storytelling. These rhythms. These dances. This beauty. This welcoming to a place where the people speak and are unafraid." —Honorée Fanonne Jeffers, author of
The Love Songs of W.E.B. Du Bois

"Hokeah skillfully recreates the years leading up to and following Ever's birth, capturing the traumas and complexities that shaped him into who he is and may determine who he becomes." —*TIME*

"Such a vital and powerful novel, giving us a wide range of voices over decades of Native life in a new and real way, from a writer I will from now on read everything he writes . . . I could not more highly recommend this book."
—Tommy Orange, author of *There There* (*Lit Hub*,
"88 Writers on the Books They Loved in 2022")

"[A] captivating debut . . . With striking insight into human nature and beautiful prose, this heralds an exciting new voice."
—*Publishers Weekly* (starred review)

"*Calling for a Blanket Dance* is a stunning novel. Oscar Hokeah writes from deep inside the heart of his communities, bringing life to generations of voices who became so real to me they felt like relatives. The reader can't help but invest in each character as they navigate bitter challenges, sometimes surprising themselves with their strength, their ability to survive and love. Hokeah's prose gorgeously weaves authentic local vernacular with the lyrical notes of hard-won insight. This novel belongs on every recommended booklist for fans of literary fiction."

—Susan Power, author of *The Grass Dancer*

"Devastating . . . A kaleidoscopic bildungsroman set against the backdrop of rural Oklahoma . . . Hokeah's characters are drawn with such precision and pathos . . . [They] exist at the intersection of Kiowa, Cherokee, and Mexican identity, which provides a vital exploration of indigeneity in contemporary American letters."

—*The New York Times Book Review*

"This miraculous story presents a collective imagining not only of who its main character is, but who everyone else anticipated and dreamed he could become. It is a must-read."   —*BuzzFeed*

"Complex histories unspool in *Calling for a Blanket Dance* . . . explor[ing] family relationships, obligation, resentment, and devotion."

—*The Boston Globe*

"Hokeah offers us a rich tapestry of interconnected narratives, a chorus of distinct voices battling against history, failing bodies, and barren landscapes. We move through decades, fall in love and despair with the Geimausaddle family. The scale and beauty remind you of *One Hundred Years of Solitude* set in Oklahoma. Here's a True American Epic."

—Gabriel Bump, author of *Everywhere You Don't Belong*

"Hokeah's prose is punchy and descriptive, filled with Native American words and phrases that come naturally to the characters. This blending of languages is still uncommon in contemporary fiction, but the current Indigenous literary and cultural renaissance promises that more voices will grow this singularity into a rich multitude. But of course, *renaissance* is the wrong word to use here. Hokeah, who is of Mexican heritage as well as a citizen of the Cherokee Nation and the Kiowa Tribe of Oklahoma, shows that this tradition has been here the whole time, evolving and surviving." —*BookPage*

"The characters that populate *Calling for a Blanket Dance* are real, amazing, vulnerable, and beautiful in their flaws, and even despair—Oscar Hokeah unveils their suffering and joy, their struggle to live with honor, care for family, walk right. What an accomplishment. Few writers have the courage or craft to pull this off. Hokeah beats the drum and stomps, announcing his power is back, the people have returned with powerful stories. He weaves a tale that is unforgettable and fortifying. I couldn't put the book down."
—Jimmy Santiago Baca, author of
A Place to Stand

"As in the novels of Louise Erdrich and Tommy Orange, the chorus of voices—rendered in unadorned vernacular peppered with Indigenous words—evokes a close-knit Native community in all its varied humanity, anchored by tradition while marked by injustices past and present . . . Simply told and true to life." —*Kirkus Reviews*

"What is wonderful about Hokeah's debut is that each character gets to tell their own story, while also covering Ever's life, who they each feel responsible for as part of their family and community . . . What we have with this book is a complete picture of one person as seen by others, and an entire community made up of Kiowa, Cherokee, and Mexican Americans, each with their own language, speech rhythms, and ways of seeing the world." —*Literary Hub*

"Oscar Hokeah is the real deal . . . A new voice with ancient music."
—Luis Alberto Urrea, author of *Good Night, Irene*

"Drawing on a wealth of Indigenous tradition, Hokeah has produced in his debut a novel that underscores the quiet strength that arises when a family is true to its identity and the too-common tragedy that results when identity is suppressed." —*The Millions*

"A masterwork of peripheral narration."
—*Kirkus Reviews* ("Best of 2022:
A Year of the 'Fully Booked' Podcast")

"Quaking with age-old righteous anger but nevertheless luminescent with hope." —*ELLE*

"[A] seamlessly woven tale . . . Hokeah peppers his quick, punchy prose with untranslated Indigenous vocabulary, which invites readers into the storytelling and binds the chapters in a shared vernacular. The result is a profound reflection on the ways familial and cultural trauma can threaten every generation while those very connections can also promise salvation." —*Booklist*

"Filled with astonishing immediacy, and embellished with Hokeah's authentic voice, these epic stories soar with indelible images of a proud but challenged people who find strength through their bloodlines and their enduring familial love. Some characters are so broken and bitter that I was moved to tears. But most characters persevere, and thrive, through the indomitable will and pride of their heritage. Hokeah has accomplished something unique here. In his quietly brilliant depiction of his Cherokee/Kiowa/Mexican heritage, he has dipped into his medicine bag and gifted us with a small but compelling masterpiece. This should be required reading for every American." —Kiana Davenport, author of *Shark Dialogues*

"A moving symphony of voices, and a beautiful story about loss and belonging." —*Book Riot*

"Hokeah's debut will feel familiar to fans of Louise Erdrich and Tommy Orange . . . A novel that builds in richness and intricacy . . . Another noteworthy debut in what feels like an ongoing renaissance of Indigenous peoples' literature, both reflecting this lineage and introducing an exciting, fresh new voice to the choir." —*Library Journal*

"Told from a variety of voices, this story is one of love, loss, growth, tradition, and evolution. Not to be missed." —*Ms.* magazine

"As a plethora of voices accompanies Ever Geimausaddle's upbringing, we learn of challenges and resilience, the multilingual language of hope, and the grace of forgiveness. Their lives, tender and difficult, full of awe and learning, remind us that the borderlands are fluid regions where families have intermingled, overcome challenges, and danced together for centuries." —Cristina Rivera Garza, author of *Grieving: Dispatches from a Wounded Country*

"An auspicious debut . . . Recalling both Tommy Orange and Gabriel García Márquez in its narrative structure . . . A book to deeply invest in." —*Chicago Review of Books*

"Oscar Hokeah is a storyteller for the ages. Wise and compassionate, *Calling for a Blanket Dance* is a gift. I couldn't put it down." —Debra Magpie Earling, author of *Perma Red*

"Remarkable." —*Shondaland*

"Hokeah's novel not only tells a story that is ultimately uplifting, but also immerses readers in Oklahoma's Kiowa, Cherokee, and Mexican communities . . . Ever and his family aren't looking for a way to define themselves within a larger national identity, but they are trying to pry their lives from the forces of generational trauma that shape their community." —*Minneapolis Star Tribune*

"Gripping; heartbreaking; hope-filled . . . Beautiful and precise and wise . . . It's wonderful; it's important." —Powell's Books

"When your heritage and ancestry are the reasons for your oppression, to whom can you turn in order to survive, but to family? Hokeah's exceptional debut novel follows a Native American man's life through the many leaves of his family tree."
—*BookPage* ("Best Fiction of 2022")

"A story of love and resiliency that is hard to put down. *Calling for a Blanket Dance* is a novel sure to remind many readers of their own families, the individuality that each person brings, the crucial role that community plays, and our interconnection."
—*Latinx in Publishing*

"A coming-of-age tale that is uniquely Kiowa and Cherokee, and that celebrates connection, family, and honor."
—Minnesota Public Radio

"Hokeah's debut novel proves the impact of generational resilience—what it means to pass down knowledge, tradition, and values . . . What sets the novel apart from a collection is that the characters refuse to stand alone, choosing to quilt their stories together. *Calling for a Blanket Dance* becomes a blanket, and, just like the stitches that bind them, it's the love for community that holds the novel together." —*World Literature Today*

CALLING FOR
A BLANKET
DANCE

CALLING FOR A BLANKET DANCE

a novel by

OSCAR HOKEAH

Algonquin Books of Chapel Hill 2023

Published by
ALGONQUIN BOOKS OF CHAPEL HILL
Post Office Box 2225
Chapel Hill, North Carolina 27515-2225

an imprint of WORKMAN PUBLISHING CO., INC.
a subsidiary of Hachette Book Group, Inc.
1290 Avenue of the Americas
New York, New York 10104

Printed in the United States of America.
Design by Steve Godwin.

The publisher is not responsible for websites
(or their content) that are not owned by the publisher.

This is a work of fiction. While, as in all fiction, the literary perceptions
and insights are based on experience, all names, characters, places, and
incidents either are products of the author's imagination or are used fictitiously.

LIBRARY OF CONGRESS CATALOGING-IN-PUBLICATION DATA
Names: Hokeah, Oscar, [date]– author.
Title: Calling for a blanket dance : a novel / by Oscar Hokeah.
Description: Chapel Hill, North Carolina : Algonquin Books of Chapel Hill, 2022. |
Summary: "A young Native American boy in a splintering family
grasps for stability and love, making all the wrong choices until
he finds a space of his own"— Provided by publisher.
Identifiers: LCCN 2022004636 | ISBN 9781643751474 (hardcover) |
ISBN 9781643752990 (ebook) | ISBN 978-1-64375-354-6 (signed edition)
Subjects: LCSH: Indians of North America—Fiction. | Families—
United States—Fiction. | LCGFT: Bildungsromans. | Novels.
Classification: LCC PS3608.O482755 C35 2022 | DDC 813/.6—dc23/eng/20220201
LC record available at https://lccn.loc.gov/2022004636

ISBN 978-1-64375-391-1 (PB)

10 9 8 7 6 5 4 3 2 1
First Paperback Edition

For my babies. Daddy loves you.

They have assumed the names
and gestures of their enemies,
but have held on to their own, secret souls;
and in this there is a resistance
and an overcoming, a long outwaiting.

—N. SCOTT MOMADAY

Geimausaddle Family

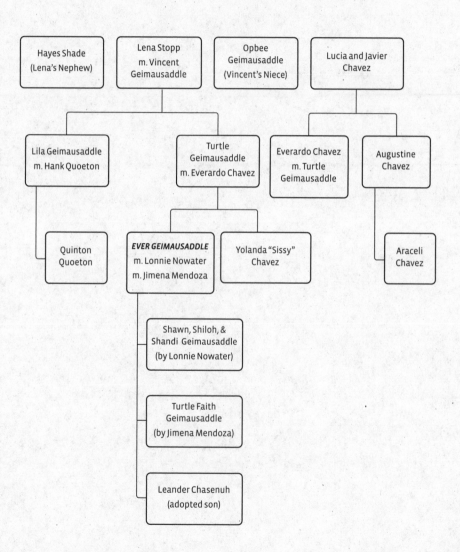

Contents

Lena Stopp (1976) 1

Vincent Geimausaddle (1981) 30

Hayes Shade (1986) 66

Lila Geimausaddle-Quoetone (1990) 83

Quinton Quoetone (1993) 94

Turtle Geimausaddle (1995) 106

Yolanda "Sissy" Chavez (1999) 118

Hank Quoetone (2003) 143

Araceli Chavez (2005) 156

Leander Chasenuh (2008) 184

Opbee Geimausaddle (2010) 202

Ever Geimausaddle (2013) 234

Acknowledgments 257

Lena Stopp
(1976)

I ALWAYS TOLD Turtle when I was raising her, "If a man acts like a child, then send him back to his ae-jee and let her straighten him out." She hardly ever listened to me—mostly, she would make a sour face and turn away—but when things got bad with Everardo, she finally did. Turtle wasn't much for talking but her emotions barked like a bluetick—you could tell. And sometimes I'd say things like, "Just because you look more Kiowa doesn't mean you can forget you're Cherokee," and she'd scrunch her brow. I'd throw back my head and laugh a good one. Tla, mostly, I liked to tease her about Everardo. The last time he stayed out all night, I told her, "That's what you get for marrying a sqaw-nee."

She'd driven around Lawton like a ski-lee on a broom-stick and found Everardo at a cousin's house half drunk and oosa-tle. She dragged him into the backseat of her car, let him pass out next to Ever—he was just six months old by then—and drove south out of Oklahoma. She headed across Texas and down into Mexico. Come to find out, Everardo hadn't seen his parents in over ten years. Turtle had just gotten her per cap money from the Kiowa Tribe, $1,500. She meant for that au-dayla to pull double duty: fixing Everardo and getting her a home.

Aldama, Chihuahua, was filled with desert and large mountain chains, unlike Lawton, which was flatter than the back of my head. There was Mount Scott just north of Lawton, but it looked more like a groundhog had dug a mound of dirt out of the Southern Plains. Turtle told me how it wasn't even a real mountain compared to the ones in Chihuahua.

As they drove into his hometown, Everardo's eyes finally popped open, with the familiar sound of dirt kicking up underneath the car. It sobered him instantly. Turtle said his face aged backward twenty years as they drove up to his parents' house. His mother, Lucia, had no idea her skee-ni son was about to arrive. I shouldn't be like that. He wasn't skee-ni. Just a selfish ouk-seni. But when Lucia opened the front door to find an older version of her baby boy, she embraced him in such a long hug that when she let go, he was five years old again.

Lucia did not waste any time. She began wrapping pork tamales, and wrapping Everardo in question after question, like about his brother, Augustine. He told her about Augustine and his new girlfriend and that they were getting married. Lucia pulled out homemade marzipan candy and shoved pieces into Everardo's mouth, feeding him like a skaw-stee little toddler. She told him about his cousins living in Riverside, California. They worked as maids in the motels and their children learned English in the schools.

My grandson, Ever, took to Lucia because she did to him what she had done to his daddy. Shoved marzipan into his mouth. Turtle said Ever scrunched up his little brow, smacked his gums a bit, and then a smile spread across his chubby face. Sure enough, he crawled into Lucia's lap like Christmas come early. The funniest part of the reunion was watching Everardo eat, or really, watching Lucia watch Everardo eat. She hadn't seen her son in a decade, so she pulled tamales from the pot and served them fresh, still steaming. Turtle said Everardo cut the smallest chunks with his fork, and slowly placed each bite onto his tongue. There he was, just like his baby, smiling from ear to ear as he chewed those tiny bites. Lucia held Ever in her lap at the kitchen table and didn't take her eyes off Everardo for a minute.

Turtle had fallen for Everardo because if he wasn't

laughing, he was smiling. Lucia told Turtle about the pranks he used to pull as a boy, how he'd trick his younger cousins into eating habaneros. Then he'd laugh as their faces turned red. One time he tied a row of firecrackers to a cat's tail. Everardo and his friends laughed until the cat ran straight into a neighbor's house. The firecrackers *did* slide off the cat's tail, but they dropped inside the living room. Everardo and his friends had to work off payments for new furniture. "This is the son that turned me into an old goat," Lucia said. She and Everardo laughed with different pitches but in the same rhythm.

His father, Javier, came home a few hours later and nearly lost his breath. He thought he saw the ghost of an ancestor, Everardo Francisco Carrillo, who was rumored to be an early Spanish governor of their hometown, Aldama. Then he nearly fainted when he realized it was a shapeshifter posing as his son. He hugged Everardo and then pulled him back by the shoulders to look at him. Hugged him again and then pulled him back again. He couldn't believe his eyes.

Javier wanted to show Everardo how his childhood home had been upgraded. New cement on the walls and floors. Then Javier took him outside to show him how he painted the cement walls pink at his mother's request. He pulled out a ladder and made Everardo climb onto the roof to see how he had personally cut the rain gutters and laid the sheet metal.

Everardo's parents had a large home—four bedrooms

with a living room and kitchen. His parents and his family had hand-built it all. Even the upgrades. It was a community effort. Turtle told me how she admired the way Everardo's family worked together to build what they needed. She listened carefully as his father explained how he used chicken wire between cement layers. There was something about the way Javier relived the building of the home. Next thing, Turtle started daydreaming. Everardo had promised her a house. One day, he always told her, over and over. But "one day" said everyday sounded more like "never."

Then Everardo's aunt stopped by to borrow sugar and coffee from his mother, and word spread like mountain winds cutting through the valley. Every night a cousin or an uncle or an old friend stopped by to visit with Everardo and to meet his wife and child. They bombarded him with questions, "What kind of work is in Oklahoma?" and "How are the cousins doing?" and "Do you have your own home?" Everardo answered accordingly, except when it came to the last. When relatives came to the question of having his own home, he told them he had a house in the middle of Lawton. According to the bull spilling out of Everardo's mouth, he had to mow the lawn all summer. "You wouldn't believe how much grass there is," he'd tell them. Everardo told them about a vegetable garden in the backyard and a flower garden off the sides of the front porch. "It's easy to grow in Oklahoma," he said, "The soil is good."

Turtle only spoke a few phrases in Spanish and a handful

of words, but she understood clearly all the bullshit Everardo told his family.

It was a lie she held for their entire trip, and it only pissed Turtle off the more she thought about not having a home of her own. She wanted nothing more than to turn the lie into truth. By time the week was over she was ready to get back to Oklahoma. On the last day, Everardo's ae-jee asked, "Just one more hug, please?" again and again. They were leaving Mexico, or trying to anyway. But Everardo couldn't deny his mother. She hadn't seen him in ten years. Lucia hugged Everardo, Turtle, and then Ever. Only to ask again right after. Then hugged them in the same order.

On the day they were to leave, Javier suddenly needed help with some last-minute work around the yard. A hole needed to be dug for a pig roast the following weekend. Then he needed help replacing a cracked window. He had Everardo hand him tools as he shimmed the busted window out and slid the new one in. When they finally climbed inside their car, tla, Lucia stopped them again. She hurried toward the house yelling, "You need this for the road." She walked back out of the house with a can of green beans and her only can opener. Everardo tried to turn it away, but his mother said, "No, no, take it." She reached inside the car window and placed the items on his lap. Then she leaned over to give him one more kiss on his forehead.

On the drive back, Peguis Canyon was wrapped inside a dark shadow, like the mountain chain was witched.

Between the growing darkness and desert, Turtle couldn't even tell which way was north. The night grew so dark it was almost like the sand itself turned black. A place where ski-lees gave birth to demons. Everardo had trekked the highway in his younger days. He seemed to know this part of Mexico well. Turtle focused all her attention on rocking Ever; she wanted him to sleep—the drive would be easier for everyone that way. Once they cleared the canyon, Everardo found a Mexican folk music station. The quick strums from a guitar mixed with a dancing violin made Ever's eyelids slowly fall. Turtle's head rolled on her neck from the long serenades between singers. Soon the darkness covering the desert looked like the darkness behind her eyelids. She tried to stay awake, pulling her eyes open and blinking repeatedly. It all started to blur. The night, the desert, the car.

Suddenly, headlights lit up the highway.

Three police cars sat parked side by side and spread across both lanes.

Everardo quickly stopped the car. Turtle didn't fully understand what was happening until she saw three Mexican policemen standing at the front of their car. She wanted to tell Everardo not to get out. But she couldn't speak. She was aus-guy. He climbed out of the car and met the policemen at the front of the vehicle. Turtle watched as he handed one of the officers his identification. This officer was the tallest of the three and wore a metal badge. The other two had similar gray uniforms, but without badges. Everardo told the badged officer he was traveling from his parents' home in Aldama, that his wife and son were in the car. Then the officer asked if he was smuggling contraband into the United States. The officer didn't wait for Everardo's response, and asked "Do you have any American money?" Everardo pulled a twenty dollar bill from his pocket, saying, "It's for gas back to Oklahoma." The badged officer snatched the twenty dollar bill out of his hand, and told Everardo to follow them back to the police station. They wanted to search the car for drugs.

Turtle said she felt sick to her stomach, and there was something skee-ni in the air. Everardo drove their car behind the badged officer while the other two police cars followed. Soon they arrived at an old, abandoned gas station just off the state highway, a converted store made into a police station. The town of Presidio was about thirty miles ahead, which meant they were only thirty miles from the U.S. border.

They huddled together outside their car, holding each other like tumbleweeds caught on a barbed wire fence. Turtle rocked her oos-di and kissed him on his cheeks. Thankfully, Ever slept. Those ou-yoee grabbed bags of clothes from the backseat and tossed them out. Next they yanked the spare tire from the trunk and threw it onto the ground. Turtle was mostly scared for Ever. She said she thought about running as fast as she could into the night. She just needed to make it to the U.S. border. Surely, the American officers would help her. She was American. Her father served in the Korean War.

Those skee-ni little assholes forced Turtle and Everardo to pick up their belongings that were strewn all over the ground. Turtle climbed into the backseat of the car and carefully laid Ever down. She was grateful when he stayed asleep. He stirred a few times as if he were hungry, but she was able to soothe him. Turtle tucked him into a blanket— not so much to keep the cold out but more to have something weighted on top of him: it always seemed to help him sleep.

Carefully, Turtle climbed out of the backseat and hurried to help Everardo pick up their clothes and stuff them back into the bags. They returned the spare tire to the trunk along with the tire jack. When she bent over to place the things into the car, she noticed those nasty policemen looking at her and smiling, like three horny desert dogs. She tried her best to hurry. She didn't like them looking at her.

Here she picked up papers that were thrown from the glove box, and she had to chase an envelope toward the policemen. "Do you want me to help you?" the badged officer asked. Turtle snatched up the envelope, hearing their coyote cackles behind her. By the time all the papers were back into the glove box, Turtle was mostly aus-guy for Ever— afraid he'd be missing—so she hurried into the backseat. She had her window down and heard the badged policeman say to Everardo, "Do you know how much money we can get for this car and all the stuff you have?"

"I'm trying to get my family back to Oklahoma," Everardo said.

The badged officer shoved Everardo to the ground. "Where's the money?"

"I don't have any more money," Everardo said, on his back and hands out.

The officer looked at Everardo's boots. "I bet I can get some money for these," he said and reached out to grab them. Everardo tried to pull his feet away but the officer caught the tip of a foot and yanked the boot off. Everardo came back around with his other foot and kicked the officer in the side of his knee. The officer stumbled and nearly fell but caught himself before he landed on the ground. Then he lunged forward and kicked Everardo in the side.

Turtle said she almost screamed but quickly held her breath. Ever was sound asleep. The last thing she needed was for him to wake up and call attention to their hiding place in the car. She wiped her tears as soon as they hit her cheeks. She looked around but could only see darkness and the police station. She knew she was close to Texas, close to the U.S. border, but not close enough to know which direction. She couldn't follow the road or else the policemen would catch her. She had a hand resting on Ever's back, and she tried her best to not cry out, to not wake him up.

On the ground, Everardo cringed against the pain in his side.

That awful badged officer pulled out his gun, smiling like a damned ski-lee, and aimed it directly at Everardo's head.

Everardo said, "No, please. My wife and son are watching, no, please."

"Maybe I'll take all of it," the officer said. "I'll sell your wife and son, too."

"God, please," Everardo begged.

The officer paused, stepped back, and holstered his gun.

Right then, Turtle told me she thought they would release Everardo. There was something about Everardo's call to God. It made the officer change. She said it seemed to frighten him. He stepped back, stood next to the other two policemen, and postured long enough to give Turtle hope. But then he yelled out into the desert and commanded the two policemen to attack. Everardo curled up into a ball as the two men sent the tips of their cowboy boots into his back, sides, and legs. Everardo used his arms to cover his head, but it didn't stop the men from stomping their heels onto his hands and arms.

"Please, stop!" Everardo yelled.

The officer pulled the two men away and he climbed on top of Everardo. He pinned Everardo's arms down with his knees and slammed his fist into Everardo's face left and right until he went unconscious, but the officer continued, Everardo's head slung around on a loose neck with each hit.

Turtle knew if they killed Everardo then she and Ever would be next. They wouldn't leave witnesses. She scooped up Ever. She got out of the car and ran *toward* the three men. Turtle slid down to her knees in front of the officer. In perfect Spanish, she said, "For God and my son, please stop. Spare us."

The badged officer was at eye level with Turtle. He paused mid swing.

Tears fell from Turtle's eyes.

Everardo's bloody face and gashed head lay between them.

Ever was now wide awake in Turtle's arms, looking out from underneath the blanket. His eyes caught the officer's eyes. He was so close to the violence, too close to the rage. Oos-dis weren't supposed to be around such things. They could be witched. Their spirit forever altered. A witching was almost incurable.

"I have money," Turtle begged, and she quickly rifled through Ever's blanket, fumbled with the snaps on his pajamas, and pulled out a tan-colored envelope, the same one that held her Kiowa per cap check. She showed the officer $1,400 in twenties and hundreds. "Take it all," she begged. "But please leave us at the border."

The officer looked at Ever in Turtle's arms and then at the wad of cash in Turtle's hands. He snatched the money, and barked at the two policemen, "Take them before I change my mind." He climbed off Everardo and walked toward the police station, using a handkerchief to wipe the blood from his knuckles.

TURTLE CALLED ME in the middle of the night. She was at a hospital in Presidio, Texas. Worse still, Everardo was nearly beaten to death. First thing I asked about was Ever. Was he okay? How was he doing? Did he see what happened to his daddy? Next thing you know Turtle barked at me, "Lena, save your superstitions for another day." Mostly, she was upset because her husband was hospitalized. Here all that they had had been stolen. Car, money, clothes, and most important, my grandson's soul. But Turtle didn't have the patience to hear the last one.

I wired Turtle money and said I'd drive down. I wanted to tell her, "I'll only send money if you come back with me to Tahlequah," but instead I said, "Don't try to leave before I get there." I also wanted to tell her, "You should've known better," meaning to go to Mexico. It wasn't America. It wasn't safe. I didn't say that either.

I held my lectures until much later, until I had them in my car, where Turtle couldn't hang up on me or walk away. The first thing I told my daughter was, "You never take an infant around violence," and she tried to argue with me, because by her take, Ever was "only" six months old and would never remember the incident. If she moved to Tahlequah, I could teach her how energy easily imprinted on the water molecules of an oos-di. Babies should be laughing and loved on. Not watching their fathers being beaten to near death. Turtle called my fears "superstitious mumbo jumbo." But it didn't stop me from telling her that Ever would need to be cured by a medicine man. When Turtle laughed, I could tell she wanted me to be offended. Then afterward, she suddenly fell dead silent. I saw the concern grow on her face. The last thing either of us wanted was for our precious oos-di to be forever witched.

Lawton was the last place I wanted to go, or wanted my daughter and grandson to go. I wanted to stay on I-44 and continue north to Oklahoma City. Then I'd turn east along I-40 so I could eventually turn north again and follow highway 69 through Muskogee. Then we would've been safely inside Tahlequah. My hometown. But Turtle jumped into the driver's seat when we stopped for gas in Wichita Falls. She said, "I'll drive the last hour to Lawton." She knew me better than most. Surely, I wouldn't kidnap my daughter and her family. Here I was offended she thought I'd try. Maybe she half expected me to make the threat, and I'd be lying if I hadn't considered it.

But I took the opportunity to refresh her memory about dirty old Lawton. It was as gada-haee as exhaust shooting out of a tailpipe, and no one cared enough to clean it. A dozen Lawtons could fit inside Oklahoma City, but it had more violent crimes. The gangs and the drugs were out of control. I hated to say it, but it was a poor town, a rat's nest, if you asked me. Fort Sill barely kept the city alive. Turtle's only reason to stay in Lawton was her daddy, Vincent, who barely took care of himself. Vincent lived off land-lease money and social security. He spent more on liquor than on his own family. And now she had a husband who lay in the backseat of my car like a sick dog. How was she going to survive? Ever had been through enough already. He didn't need to be exposed to more of the same. Better yet, I could call on a medicine man to have Ever cured.

Instead Turtle focused on driving and didn't say a word to me. Her face flushed, and the red in her cheeks nearly boiled to a purple. There was a second reason to stay in Lawton, her sister, Lila. But she wasn't going to be any help. She had a family of her own. "How was she going to take on a whole other family?" I asked her. Again, Turtle pretended to not hear. Sadly, my warnings didn't stop her from pulling off I-44 and onto Lee Boulevard, so I began to plead, telling her how I'd give her the money that was stolen, but only if she came with me to Tahlequah. I didn't even deny Everardo. "Bring him, too," I told her.

It would've been better to get a snide answer, but Turtle wasn't built that way. She drove us through Lawton and pulled up to Vincent's house, letting me sulk like a ten-year-old. I'll give her this: her silence was precise and cut perfectly into the heart.

"What's wrong with Everardo?" I asked. I knew he was

beaten but there was more, something she wouldn't say. It took us both to help him into Vincent's house, and she finally said, "It's his kidneys. He's still peeing blood." I was shocked because it was the first time I realized how deeply Everardo was wounded. Suddenly, I realized that his damaged kidneys could turn into a permanent disability. Now I truly understood the depth of Turtle's concern—not only for the health of her husband, but for their future raising a family.

Sure enough, Vincent wasn't home, and Turtle told me how he disappeared as soon as his Kiowa per cap check arrived. I wasn't surprised. I also wasn't surprised to step into his little one-bedroom house to find it in such sad condition. There were no decorations on the walls, dust stood an inch thick on every surface, and his kitchen was littered with dishes. It was likely in as sad a condition as Vincent himself, but he wasn't around to compare. We helped Everardo into Vincent's bed, and Turtle situated the pillows just right. A glass of water. Pain pills.

Ever kept me busy by constantly crawling into the kitchen and then the bathroom. To distract him, I handed him one of Vincent's gourd rattles. Ever sat in the middle of the living room holding the rattle and swung the metal tin shaker repeatedly over his head, as if he were calling to the birds. I couldn't help but laugh at how much he reminded me of Vincent. The way Vincent held his eagle feather fan and gourd rattle during the dances. He'd almost cross the two just above his head, his knees bent low with each drop to the drumbeat. It was easy to fall in love with Vincent—he was like a drug—but I hadn't known what I was getting myself into until it was already too late.

And there I sat in Vincent's living room. A part of me wanted to wait long enough to watch him walk through the door. The part that remembered his dance, and his sideways glances laced with a playful cockiness. Maybe I still loved him. But not enough to forget the pain, like his absence, like the emptiness of this home. I watched Turtle zip into the kitchen and then back to the bedroom, rummage through a closet and then back to the bedroom, and then hurry into the bathroom and then back to the bedroom. Then I looked down at Ever, shaking his grandfather's rattle. That's when I understood Turtle was still caught in Everardo's dance. The way I had been caught in Vincent's. She wouldn't leave Everardo any more than an alcoholic could leave alcohol. So I picked up Ever, kissed him hard on the check, and told him, "Make your momma bring you to me. I'll get you a medicine man." I laughed at his big, bright eyes.

Then I handed Ever to Turtle, and told her, "When you're ready to move to Tahlequah, call me."

IT WAS DURING one of our rare phone calls when Vincent explained to me how he came home a week later and found Everardo lying in his bed. Vincent told me how Turtle was nowhere to be seen, and neither was Ever. Vincent stood in the doorway to his own bedroom. He and Everardo locked eyes.

Vincent asked, "Where's my daughter?"

Everardo was tucked under Vincent's Pendleton blanket and responded in Spanish. Vincent had no idea what he said. He walked into the living room and laughed at himself for being unable to go into his own room. Vincent took sympathy when he saw how badly Everardo was beaten. The bruises were likely fading and becoming yellow, but the majority of his face had to have been swollen and gashed, and even if the swelling was modest at that point it'd still be enough to frighten anyone who suddenly crossed him. By that evening, Vincent started to worry if Turtle had abandoned Everardo all together, left him lying in her father's bed as a sort of odd revenge on them both. Vincent told me how he laughed at the idea of Turtle forcing the two men in her life to deal with each other. Turtle had her ways. She might not tear you apart like a tornado, but she knew how to bend you with the lightest breeze. But he became more and more frustrated as each minute passed. Here he was trapped inside his own house, of all things.

Finally, Turtle walked through the door, and quickly apologized as soon as she saw her daddy. She sat Ever in the middle of the living room with his toys but kept apologizing as she did so.

Vincent barked, "What the hell is going on?" He not

only wanted to know what was happening with Everardo but also why she would leave him all day in such condition.

Turtle had landed a job at a department store called TG&Y, where she stocked the clothing racks, and already loved the job. Specifically, she loved not cutting and pulling weeds in the peanut and cotton fields, like she and Everardo had been doing. The new job inspired her to do something she had never done before. She asked a local bank for a home loan. Turtle said the loan manager was a stalky man with eyeglasses nearly as large as his face. She walked in with Ever on her hip. Ever was hard to resist—he had something about him that drew people. I'd like to think it was those Cherokee curls. I can just see how Ever sat patiently in his momma's lap as she asked about the home loan. The loan manager would've given Ever some candy, I'm sure. Everyone wanted to give Ever something. In this case, someone wanted to give his mother a loan for a house.

Turtle just needed to raise $2,000.

"I don't have that kind of money," Vincent told Turtle when she asked him for help.

"Not the full two thousand, just part of it," she said. She had planned to work for the bulk of the money. "What happened to all your per cap money?"

Vincent's face turned sour and he said, "What kind of criminal stuff is he into? Somebody attacked him and now you want him to stay in my home. And why are you asking me about my per cap? What happened to yours?!"

Ever had been on the living room floor until Vincent started yelling. Then he turned aus-guy and crawled over to Turtle. She pulled him onto her lap. Turtle told her father about what happened to Everardo and how I'd driven down and picked them up at the Mexican border. Then she told him, "We've been staying with you all this time. We have nowhere to go. And you want to kick your grandson out onto the streets?" She just needed time to get the money together.

"He has a brother and cousins," Vincent said. "The ones he gets drunk with."

"Why would I take him there?" Turtle pleaded with her father, asking for just one month. If anything, just enough time to pay for a house. Then she'd never have to ask him for anything again.

Vincent sat on the edge of his recliner and fumed. He was silent for a few minutes. Turtle said he shook his head and quickly stood, saying, "One month." Then he stormed into his bedroom and pulled clothes from the drawers and closet. He threw them into a plastic trash bag and carried the bag out of the house without saying another word to Turtle, not even saying goodbye to his grandson.

A FEW DAYS later Augustine arrived on the doorstep and *demanded* to see his brother, as if Turtle had been keeping him hostage. Bullshit. Here she juggled an injured husband and a baby who recently learned to crawl. If not for Lila, she wouldn't have been able to hold her job at TG&Y. Turtle let him inside and pointed to the bedroom. It was Everardo who told him, "Turtle was the one who made me call our parents." Otherwise, Augustine wouldn't have even known Everardo had been attacked. So much for keeping anyone hostage.

Everardo was ashamed and humiliated by it all, I suppose. He had stayed away from his family because he didn't want anyone to see him beaten and bruised. He looked like an old patched road with potholes and felt like one, too. His kidneys hurt, and until recently he had only been able to walk as far as the living room, where he spent a few hours each day. Augustine slowly approached the bed and sat next to his brother. Everardo looked away. He said, "Please leave. I'm tired. I'll call you when I can work again."

Augustine had always driven him, along with other migrant farmers, to the peanut and cotton fields north of Lawton.

Turtle said Augustine asked in Spanish what was wrong with Everardo, how long it would take him to recover. Turtle explained in English that his kidneys were so damaged he might not be able to work again. Then she watched Augustine's face turn to sadness as his head dropped. A deep sound suddenly rose from his chest. Finally, he sighed in defeat. There was nothing he or anyone could do. Everardo just had to heal.

Turtle tried to reassure Augustine and told him how she

had her new job at TG&Y. She was working toward a loan for a new home. "I'll provide for Everardo if he can't work." She wanted to show Everardo's family how much she loved him, and that she wouldn't abandon him just because he was sick.

In English, Augustine said, "We provide the home."

Turtle said, "Your brother isn't less of a man because he's hurt."

But Augustine either didn't understand Turtle or didn't want to give her the satisfaction.

It was two days later when Augustine showed up at the door again. This time he had an envelope with cash. He didn't ask to see his brother. He stood at the front door and handed Turtle the envelope, saying, "Our mother and father in Mexico want this for you."

After she shut the door, she quickly opened the envelope and found $500 in random bills. Most of it was U.S. currency but some of it was Mexican. Everardo's parents must have taken up a collection from family and friends in Aldama, but likely most of it came from family in the U.S.

This is where Turtle got the crazy idea to call me, and I should've known by the softness in her voice she was buttering me up for something. Somehow I was caught off guard when she said, "Remember how you offered to give me the money that was stolen?" I remembered, but it was under the condition that she move to Tahlequah. Here she said,

"Instead," and asked for $500, but she'd be staying in Lawton. "It's a smaller amount," she told me.

"Only if you look for a house in Tahlequah," I said. That was the deal. Cherokee Nation was building Indian Homes north of Sequoyah High School. If she moved right away, she might be able to get into a newly built home. Instead of getting a loan for an older one.

"I don't want to live in Tahlequah," she told me.

"It's better than Lawton."

"I don't want to live around Cherokees," Turtle barked at me, and added, "Cherokees are mean. Especially the full-bloods."

I laughed at her, and said, "Kiowas are skaw-stee little snobs and too sensitive for any good Cherokee to deal with. Turtle, since you're half, what does that make you?"

She hung up the phone.

I'm not proud of that. Right after I heard the receiver click, I realized I had just proved her point. So maybe Turtle was right about full-blood Cherokees, or at least she was right about me.

Soon enough, Turtle called in reinforcements. Her sister, Lila, gave me an earful, too. She wanted to know what was wrong with Lawton. To save myself from having two daughters at my throat, I refrained from telling Lila what I had told Turtle, that Lawton was a place where desperate people lived. Instead I talked about how Tahlequah had Northeastern State University and Cherokee Nation to keep the town healthy. We were the county seat, too. So there were intersections of various police forces in our area, between county, city, and highway patrol. Not to mention we were a small town, the way people dreamed of small towns. No one locked their doors. The biggest ruckus came from the Illinois River on the weekends primarily, because the college kids liked to drink too much beer. No place was without its problems, but Tahlequah didn't have an infestation of gangs and drugs.

"Me and Hank are giving Turtle $500," Lila announced, like she wanted the comment to slap me in the face. It was more like a boot kick to the head. I'd be lying if I said it didn't hurt, but mostly because I had angered both my daughters. Why and how could they blame me for trying to get them to move closer? Certainly, they understood. There wasn't much I could do about Lila. She and her husband already moved into their "forever home." My only chance came with Turtle. It was a small window and I was only getting older. Vincent didn't see past the wis-gi bottle in his hands; teaching his grandkids about Kiowa culture and history was the last thing on his mind. Maybe I only spoke phrases and words in Cherokee, but I attended Stomp Dances, and if he lived near me, Ever could lead his own Stomp by the time he was five years old. My legs weren't as strong as they once were, but I had switched from the heavier turtle shells to the lighter can shells, so I could lead a Stomp Dance right along with him. Imagine the things I could teach him. Besides, what was a grandmother without her grandchildren?

Turtle, like Lila, seemed to care little about a grandmother's suffering, and she raised her portion of the loan money at TG&Y in four weeks. Everardo now moved around the house better, sitting in the recliner and cooking in Vincent's kitchen. After a month of chasing wis-gi with his friends, Vincent returned to claim his home, but she was still short $500. Again, when Vincent walked in, he found himself sitting in his own house waiting for Turtle to get off work. He and Everardo stared at each other. Everardo nodded. Then Vincent nodded back. There was really nothing more the two could do with each other.

Vincent's call came as a surprise. I hadn't spoken to him directly since Ever was born, and even then, it was more of a "half-assed osiyo." Since our children were adults, there was little to no reason to speak to each other.

Vincent sounded desperate. "Lena, you have to help her out."

"What about your per cap?" I asked him, but I knew the answer. There was a little part of me that wanted him to squirm. Well, maybe a big part of me.

"I drank it up, Lena!" Vincent yelled, "You know that. Does that make you happy?"

It did. But I said, "That's not why I asked," which was a lie. "I thought you might have a little left and then maybe I could help with the remainder." I caught myself smiling—good thing this conversation happened over the phone.

I said, "Tell her to move to Tahlequah." I could drive down to pick them up and had already started thinking about a day on the weekend to make the trip, but he laughed into the phone.

"No one wants to live in Tahlequah," he told me. I braced myself for the "mean Cherokees" comment, but Vincent said Cherokee County only had hound dogs, raccoons, and red ferns. He had recently watched the movie *Where the Red Fern Grows* and laughed from beginning to end. Hillbillies, he called us. Sure the movie was filmed around Tahlequah, but there was more to us than Ozark Hills.

"The girls know you have the money," he said. Certainly, I did well, selling hand-stitched quilts. Enough to pay all my bills and start a savings account. I wasn't much for going out. The occasional Stomp Dance was my biggest venture, and mostly I did that to catch up with friends and family, and I've never been one to pass up a hog fry at the Stomp. Couldn't go wrong with good food. This only cost me gas money to get out toward Vian. I lived modestly and had more interest in making my quilts than anything else. It felt good to know I helped someone stay warm in the winters, and then there was the look of awe when people saw my quilts. If anything, I liked giving people a sense of safety. And quilts were important for healing. Folks were willing to pay a lot of money for mine.

Vincent said, "If you don't help, the girls will never forget."

Thankfully, I had just completed an order for an oil-rich family in Tulsa. Here they offered to pay double price. Each blanket fetched $100 normally so $1,000 for five blankets was more than enough. If I gave Turtle the money, then maybe she could give Lila back hers. Then the girls would be satisfied. I'd rather have daughters who never visited because they were busy, rather than have daughters who never visited because they hated me.

And then I thought: What if I made a special quilt for Ever? A grandchild quilt. I could use a bird pattern so he would always remember he belonged to the Bird Clan. Then I had another idea: to make one for all my grandchildren and great grandchildren as they were born. It would keep our clan traditions alive in the family. My mind raced with excitement. It was a way to have them close even though they might never be. Great ideas always came in threes, so a third one hit me. I could have the quilt blessed by a medicine man. I'd tell the medicine man about Ever being there when his father was attacked. My grandson absorbed all that negativity from those skee-ni men. It might be the only way to cure Ever before fear and anger set too deep inside his spirit.

I took a full week to sew Ever's quilt.

What was one more week?

The day after I finished Ever's quilt I packed all the blankets into my car and drove to Tulsa. The family gushed over the patterns and colors. They looked closely at the stitches, running their fingers over the thread. It was a couple with three kids. The children immediately wrapped the quilts around their shoulders and started running around the house. Not only did I get my double price, but I also received a little tip. It was enough to pay for my trip across Oklahoma. I left Tulsa and headed south toward Lawton. A few hours later, I pulled into Vincent's driveway.

"They moved out," he told me.

Because of Everardo's poor health, Augustine made a special trip to Mexico and brought their parents up to see him. Everardo was so excited to see his parents again and he bragged on Turtle to no end, how she was a *saint* for saving his life and then nurturing him back to health. Lucia and Javier pulled off a miracle to match. They raised the last $500 from family and friends. Out of pure gratitude, his parents wanted to help buy their first home.

As I drove up to Turtle's house, there was a crowd of people in the driveway. Everardo's family. His mother and father. His brother with his girlfriend. Turtle stood on the front porch. Lucia held Ever in her arms. She ran a hand through his curls. Then she kissed Ever on his cheek, only to reach over and give Everardo a kiss on his cheek right after. They were saying goodbye. I kept driving. The blessed quilt I made for Ever sat on my front seat. The money I brought laid on top.

As I drove by, Turtle saw me, locked eyes with me, and

I saw her looking for my defeat. I tightened my brow and narrowed my eyes. Driving out of Lawton, I laid my hand onto Ever's quilt and traced my fingertips around the edges of the bird pattern. I couldn't help but wonder, tla, couldn't help but worry: Would my grandson ever be cured?

Vincent Geimausaddle

(1981)

SIX DAYS SOBER and the details were so crisp I finally saw stains on my dirty sheets. Bay'gaw! Six days wasn't very long. But I was a'daw, drunk daw, to wake up and fall asleep. Suddenly, people were no longer like ghosts floating around me. I stared at the coffee when I poured it from the canister into the coffee machine. I ran my fingers over the laces on my tho'days. Gaa, I had to laugh at myself. What was I doing? Guess I saw the world again, like new, or maybe this was the first time. The only bad parts were the headaches and tremors. I had felt those before and drank to calm the withdrawals. This time I had reasons to face the nerves, to face the pain, to face so many things, like who I had become.

It was on my sixth day sober when my youngest daughter, Turtle, stopped by. I lived down the road from Mattie Beal Park in Lawton, about a block toward Roosevelt Elementary School. She had Ever with her. Sissy had a cousin on her daddy's side who was her same age, and she spent most of her time over there. Ever was a different story. He trailed behind his momma like a hungry little bird. I couldn't help but laugh at him.

As soon as Turtle stepped into the house, she said, "Did you see your lease man?" And I knew what she wanted. The only time I saw my daughters was after the first of the month—right after I received money for the twenty acres of land in my name just north of Carnegie. It was leased to a farmer who grew peanuts and cotton.

Ever hid behind Turtle's legs. His head full of curls, like his momma. His grandma, my Lena, had thick, curly hair, like a lot of Cherokees in Tahlequah, because of the Irish in their bloodline. Ever was the only boy in the family with hair like that.

And he was as mean as any of them. I said, "Aim'ah," and he turned his head away. I playfully grabbed for his arm. Most of my grandkids called out to their mothers for help. This one? He turned and punched me in my hand. A full-on punch. I laughed at him. I told him, "I'm your kown."

He just stayed behind his mother's legs and stared at me with a hard scowl. His mother laughed. I laughed. Then I paused and she paused. She looked at me a little harder.

"I haven't had anything to drink in six days," I said.

I didn't remember the last time we laughed together. I usually laughed at her. Teased her too much. Mostly, about being too fat or too quiet. "No one even knows you're around," I'd told her, or "Gaa, buy men's shirts already." I wanted to tell her I was sorry. I don't know why I couldn't. Instead, I pulled out my wallet and gave her all I had left—one hundred dollars. I wasn't going to need it anyway. You couldn't take these things with you to the grave.

Turtle made her way toward the door, but before Ever hurried outside, might know, he turned and showed me his balled-up fist. Shot me a glare, too, like a little caged bird ready to tear into my fingers. Turtle and I both threw our heads back and laughed a good one.

After they left, I sat in my recliner and I ran the memories through my mind: Ever punching me in my hand, Turtle laughing with me, and Ever holding his little fist in the air. I couldn't remember the last time I had sat in my recliner, sipped on some coffee, and just remembered my family. That's when I realized I didn't have memories anymore. The alcohol had taken them from me. Too, it stole moments from my daughters and grandchildren. When you invited the spirit of something into your body, it took over.

Turtle knocked on my door two days later, and I was

surprised to see her sister, Lila, standing next to her, both with their boys. Ever walked into the house with Turtle, and Lila had brought Quinton. Ever and Quinton were both around five years old. I think Quinton had a few months on Ever, but not much. Together they took turns jumping off the arms of my couch. Lila kept Quinton's hair long and it ran down the length of his back. No ponytail. His hair flew every direction when he jumped. Ever had those curls people wanted to run their fingers through, but he drew back when someone extended a hand toward him.

It was Lila who said it. "I didn't believe Turtle when she told me." They had stopped by my house to see if old mon'sape was still sober. I was. Eight days with no whiskey. How did I remember? Because the boys wanted to go in my bedroom, and I wouldn't let them. I always did well to keep my living room clean. My couch and love seat were faded and I didn't have anything hanging on my walls. But I managed to keep my small house ordered and in pretty good shape. The bedroom told a different story. I still had empty bottles of Southern Comfort on the dresser and nightstand. If someone lifted the edges of the quilt, they would see a wasteland of empty bottles underneath the bed. The half pints I threw into the bottom drawer of my dresser. I never had the energy to dump them all into a trash bag and carry them out to the curb. Why did I let them build up? A full whiskey bottle was as light as air. Real easy to lift to my lips. An empty? It weighed like a mountain; the idea of picking it up exhausted me. Maybe I wanted someone to find them and rescue me. But Sayn'day must've known I didn't deserve rescuing, because it never happened.

I stopped the boys by telling them, "I have a surprise for you!" I knew I had some orange sherbet pushups and dug them out of the freezer. The boys took one each and ran outside to eat on the front porch. Turtle and Lila had them leave the front door open to keep an eye from my couch.

I planted myself onto my tattered recliner. "So you came to see the miracle?"

"We were afraid you might be dying," Turtle said, and the two of them laughed.

I didn't so much as laugh as chuckle. I said, "Only a little every day." I followed it with another chuckle and we all three pretended laughter. I wanted to tell them about my unexpected trip to Lawton Indian Hospital eight days before. I almost did. But I looked at them sitting on my couch and liked seeing their smiling faces. My grandsons sat on the porch silently working on their pushups. I paid special attention to the moment because I wanted to remember; I liked remembering and felt the memory form almost as each second passed. I didn't want any more bad memories or empty spaces. I'm sure I gave my family enough of those. So I held my tongue and laughed or pretended to laugh. When we're faced with our own mortality the only strength we have left is laughter. Besides, I had been selfish enough and didn't have the taste to beg for pity.

"Can you still drive?" Turtle asked me.

I had my old Apache truck parked in the driveway. It was red and rusted but the rust matched the red. It had a good carburetor, but the gas pedal needed a few hard pumps before it kicked over. I was like that before my morning coffee.

"I drive it to Discount Grocery every week," I told them.

There was a reason Turtle and Lila stopped by. It had to do with Everardo. He had collapsed at work a couple days before. He worked at a butcher shop. There was a biting pain in his lower back all morning, and just as he cut into a leg quarter to slice another sirloin, he paused, grabbed his lower back, and dropped down to his knees.

His supervisor saw him collapse and ran up to his side.

"No, no," Everardo barked and pulled himself back to his feet. He proceeded to finish cutting the sirloin.

His supervisor took the butcher knife out of his hand and said, "This is a safety concern, Everardo." Might know, he was sent home. But Everardo was one of those workaholics so he went back to work the next day, claiming to feel better. Turtle said he had been awake all night and curled in a ball. He moaned and rolled from side to side. She said his entire body hurt and she begged to take him to the hospital, but he refused. Stubborn guy. The next morning, Everardo lasted an hour, probably less. Sure enough, his supervisor sent him away again.

This time Turtle drove him straight to Comanche County Memorial Hospital and wouldn't hear nothing different. He was so bad she had to half carry him into the emergency room. He was at a point where he couldn't walk. He kept complaining that his entire body ached. The worst of the pain was in his stomach and lower back.

The receptionist told them, "He can't be admitted here."

"Look at him," Turtle said. She held his arm around her shoulders. Most of his weight was on Turtle's body. His skin was clammy, and he shivered from an uncontrollable fever.

"He doesn't have any insurance."

She drove Everardo across town to the Indian Hospital. Since Everardo was Mexican, she was sure they would turn him away. But she was bent on begging, if it came to it. Too, Everardo was curled up in the passenger seat and moaning against the pain in his body. "I don't know," he kept saying, then, "Help me."

In the Indian Hospital parking lot, she tried to lift Everardo out of the passenger seat. But it didn't work out. His entire weight came down on her. She couldn't hold him up. He tumbled to the ground outside the car door. One of the ER nurses rushed a wheelchair into the parking lot and helped Everardo climb inside.

"He's Mexican," she told the nurse.

"That doesn't matter here," he told Turtle. "He's your husband."

Good thing, too, because Everardo grew worse by the second. They took him straight to a room and helped him onto a hospital bed. Everardo curled up and could barely straighten out his arm for the nurses to draw blood.

Within half an hour, a doctor walked into their room and

told Turtle, "He's dying." It was the last thing she wanted to hear. His kidneys, they told her. They had stopped working and his body was filling with poison. They called an ambulance to transport Everardo to St. Anthony Hospital in Oklahoma City.

And now it was the afternoon, and Turtle had a small window of time before the ambulance would leave.

"We have a favor to ask," Lila said. Turtle usually got the boys from their kindergarten class at Roosevelt Elementary School. Her supervisor at TG&Y allowed her to work a split shift on weekdays. Once Lila got off from Sears, Turtle would return to work. Sissy stayed with her cousin since Everardo's sister-in-law stayed home with her kids. But my daughters needed someone to pick up the boys from school while Turtle was in Oklahoma City with Everardo.

"The school is only a few blocks away," I told them. "Won't be a problem."

"And you're not drinking?" Turtle asked.

"Haven't been," I said.

"Well, this isn't the time to start back up," Lila said.

I couldn't agree with her more. I could've explained to her how and why I wouldn't be buying any more bottles, but I still found the words caught somewhere between guilt and self-hatred.

THE WEEK BEFORE Everardo had his kidney failure, I'd had my own unexpected trip to the Indian Hospital. In the middle of the night, I took a trip to the restroom, but I didn't make it back to my bed. The next morning, I woke up on the floor. Old people fainted, so I thought nothing of it. I was an old man, and my body wasn't as strong as it once was. I had probably stood up too fast, I told myself.

But then I felt a tiredness where I couldn't even think. My body was so completely exhausted I couldn't find answers to the smallest things: Should I get dressed? or What am I going to eat? Too, the next day I tried to get some extra sleep so I stayed in bed; might know, I didn't even have the energy to pull a whiskey bottle out of a drawer. Gaa, I woke up the following day and found my stomach had swollen. I'm a fit person and have been my entire life. I'm one of those lucky guys who needed to eat five meals a day to survive. Then suddenly my stomach was coming out over my beltline. Bay'gaw! Between my big bote, the fall, and being so exhausted, I thought I better get into my truck and drive myself to the hospital.

"You're also jaundiced," a doctor told me in the emergency room. He flashed a light into my eyes and listened to my breathing. When he came back into the room an hour later, he had a nurse with him. He said, "Your blood tests show elevated enzymes and proteins in your liver."

As soon as he said liver, my head dropped. I looked away. He kept talking. But I didn't care. He overexplained the way doctors liked to do. The nurse wouldn't look at me.

"Vincent," the doctor called out. "Are you okay?"

"Tell me how long," I said.

He dropped his arms, glanced at the nurse, and then pulled up a chair. "Given the levels of enzymes and proteins in your bloodstream we have to classify you as high risk."

I think he wanted me to say something. But I just stared at him.

"Do you have family with you here today?"

I shook my head.

He didn't want to tell me. The way he hesitated. Maybe it was because he was a young doctor who hadn't gotten his legs for delivering bad news, maybe I was the first, or maybe he thought a relative could console me. I wasn't sure, but it took him a few seconds to look me in the eye and say, "Vincent, I'm sorry. You have cirrhosis." He paused, looked at his clipboard, and then back up at me. "It's in its final stage."

I must have made a noise, a "hmm," or something along those lines. He looked at me like I might speak, so I asked, "How long do I have?"

"It's a fifty percent chance you survive the next twelve months."

THE DIURETICS TOOK down the swelling in my stomach and feet, but there was nothing they could do about the cirrhosis. The fact was this: I had an end date. Life was unpredictable and it allowed us to stay sane. The unpredictability helped us believe we had an infinite number of days. If I told someone they were going to die in twelve months, they might do something incredibly stupid, or they might decide to take the remaining time to make things right. Now, when I was alone in my house, I wanted to just finish it, drink myself to death. Zadle'bay! I wanted to run to a liquor store. A couple times I tried. But haw'nay, I'd stop myself at my front door. My thoughts swayed for a week. Should I just do it? Get a'daw one last time. Go for a full liter like I used to when I was young. Just end it all. Then Turtle and Lila came to me about watching my grandsons. It was enough to calm those urges.

The day after Everardo was transported to Oklahoma City was my first chance to make up for lost time. I pulled into the car line in front of Roosevelt Elementary School. As my Apache truck stuttered and spurted in idle, I looked at the crowd of kids streaming out of the front door. Ever and Quinton walked out together—shoulder to shoulder—like Half Boys. One of the teachers walked over and asked me, "Who are you here for?"

"My grandsons," I told her, and the sound of those words coming out of my mouth nearly choked me up.

"Are you Ever and Quinton's grandfather?" she asked and didn't wait for me to answer. "They've been talking about you all day."

"This is my grandpa!" Ever yelled to the teacher, and she chuckled at his enthusiasm. The boys jumped into my truck and sat right next to me. I couldn't help but stare at them for a moment. Maybe I was trying to create a memory, something I could hold on to after they left, or maybe

I was trying to create a memory for them, something they could hold on to after I left. But they appeared so tiny sitting there. They looked up at me with the same eyes. I looked for myself in their faces and lost myself for a moment.

"Thank you, Grandpa," the teacher called out—more to get me moving.

I shifted the truck into drive and pulled away from the school.

"Look what followed me from the freezer," I said, pointing at two pushups on the seat. They yelled and Ever snatched up the pushups, handing one to Quinton. As they worked on their treats, I drove over to Mattie Beal Park. It was only a few blocks from the school and about a block from my house. We sat in the truck as they slowly pushed the sherbet up and licked off the top.

"I want to ask you boys something," I said.

"Okay," they said in unison.

"What tribe are you?"

"What's that?" Ever asked. Quinton just kept tearing into his sherbet.

"Your grandpa is Kiowa," I said. "That's my tribe. So that means you're Kiowa."

"Is that like a Indian?" Quinton asked. His lips turned more and more orange.

"Yes, Kiowa is a kind of Indian," I told them.

"My mom is a Cherokee," Ever said, and Quinton quickly echoed, "My mom is, too."

"Your moms are Kiowa and Cherokee," I tried to explain,

and I knew at this point I was in a losing battle. But old men like to be right, so I asked them, "Did you know your moms are my daughters?"

They didn't seem to care; their focus was on the orange sherbet.

"Have you guys been to a gourd dance?" I asked them. "Do you know what that is?"

"Some of the older kids at school like to break dance," Ever said. "They saw it in a movie."

"I don't know what that is," I told them. "But a gourd dance is for Kiowas."

"The kids at school wear parachute pants," Quinton said. "I guess it helps them break when they dance."

"Kiowas always wear red on the left," I told them. I wanted to teach them about their culture. I knew Turtle and Lila were always busy with work. I didn't know how much time they spent at the gourd dances.

"What color do Cherokees wear?" Ever asked.

"Cherokees don't have a color."

"Mom is *not* going to like that," Quinton added.

"No, I mean in the gourd dances there are two colors. Red for Kiowa and blue for Comanche."

"My dad's a Comanche," Quinton said. He was almost to the end of his Popsicle.

"Your dad is Kiowa and Comanche," I told Quinton.

"Do Mexicans have a color?" Ever asked.

"No, Mexicans don't have a color."

"How come I saw three colors on a big blanket at my house?" Ever asked. "Red, white, and green."

"That was a flag, Ever."

"What about Indians?" Quinton asked. "What color do Indians have?"

"My favorite color is blue," Ever said, and Quinton echoed, "Me, too."

It was odd how easily those little boys defeated an old man. I squeezed my grip on the steering wheel and shook my head. I've always had a full head of black hair, but I swear it could've all turned gray after trying to talk to them boys about being Kiowa. All I had left in me was to bark at them, "Aren't you done with those pushups yet? Hurry up and go play."

After I handed the boys off to Lila, I marched into my house and went straight for my kitchen. I yanked open a drawer and pulled out a box of black plastic trash bags. I took the box into my bedroom and used my arm to sweep a dozen empty pints of Southern Comfort off my dresser, letting them drop into a trash bag, sending out sharp pitches of glass-on-glass. I cringed but the sound made me feel good and I wanted more. Same with the empties on my night-stand. I plucked bottles off my bedroom floor, like pulling weeds. I lifted the quilt from around the edges of my bed and I jabbed a broom to push out empty pints, fifths, and liters. After a while, I grew tired, and I sat on the edge of my bed. Once my energy returned, I picked up the broom and went after those empties again. I was probably picking up bottles for an hour between all my breaks. By the time I was done I had two trash bags filled with dead whiskey bottles lying on my bedroom floor like body bags. I paused at the thought and then suddenly wanted the bags out of my room.

I grabbed one bag by its top and dragged it out of the bedroom, across the living room, and out my front door. It left a line of whiskey on the floor. I didn't care. Bottles broke against the cement on the front steps. I paused every few steps to catch my breath, but I didn't quit until both bags were on the curb next to the trashcan.

I found an old bottle of Pine-Sol and mopped the floors in my living room, kitchen, bathroom, and bedroom until they were spotless. I took a minute to rest, but I wasn't completely wiped out. Next thing I knew I was in my closet opening up boxes I hadn't been inside of for years.

As I pulled out old clothes, might know, I ran into a small white box I hadn't thought about in years. I opened the top of the box and looked at the stack of medals from the Korean War. I'd been stationed in Japan when they called us over to Korea. I found a picture at the bottom of the box. It was of me as I sat in front of a Japanese tapestry, a cigarette in my hands. I was looking away from the camera and caught with a half-smile. Must have been a month or so before the conflict began. Gaa, I stared at the picture for a while, trying to remember ever being such a young guy. I ran a finger over the multicolored medals in the box. My

Purple Heart sat on top of the others, like dead bodies on top of each other in a ditch, like empty shell casings stacking at my feet, like a pile of fucking screams tearing at my ears. I fucking hated war! Haw'nay, I fucking hated people. More, I hated myself. I slammed the lid shut on the box. It was my time, finally. My time to rotate home.

THAT WEEK, TURTLE told me how TG&Y wanted to fire her for missing two weeks of work. What kind of people didn't have a heart for what she was going through? Zadle'bay! But her supervisor stuck up for her and told the store manager how Turtle did as much work as three people. Luckily, they allowed her to stay. But she didn't want to make any more waves. If she lost her job, they'd lose their house.

"We've been there five years," she told me. It was where both Ever and Sissy learned to walk. They had their own rooms. But I think she cried harder for the decades they wouldn't have. Who was she without a home? Her house made her feel safe. It was where she kept her children safe. A house, like land, taught us how to belong and who we belonged to. If she lost herself, what did that mean for her children?

And she'd nearly lost Everardo. His blood pressure had been elevated for years due to old injuries to his kidneys. Now they'd both shut down, and he went for dialysis treatments three times a week. Then he'd get sick afterward.

It was around a week after Everardo's discharge when

Turtle received a letter from St. Anthony's Hospital, stating his "permanent physical disability," and she found herself defeated. The first Monday back to Lawton, she drove Everardo to Comanche County Dialysis Center and waited until they had him hooked to a machine, a tube going into one side of his left arm and another running out a different vein on the same arm. He leaned back in the chair and closed his eyes—he would be hooked to the machine for the next four hours. Turtle left and drove to the Comanche County Department of Human Services building with the letter. They helped her fill out some forms. By the time Everardo was done with his treatment, Turtle had received a temporary emergency check from the welfare office. The following Wednesday went the same. While Everardo's blood pumped through the dialysis machine, Turtle drove herself across Lawton *again*, but this time to the Social Security Office. Between welfare and social security, Turtle found a way to keep from losing her house.

AFTER TWO WEEKS of having Ever and Quinton every day, Turtle asked me, "Could you keep picking them up on Monday, Wednesday, and Friday?" To be honest, I smiled like the boys: big and goofy. I told her I could help with the boys as late as she needed.

"They take care of me more than I take care of them," I said and laughed.

If the boys were going to learn their culture, I'd have

to get my old ass out of the house. Who else was going to take them to the dances? Turtle couldn't. Lila worked long hours. If I took the boys, my daughters could have a little more time to themselves and get their business in order. Besides, it gave me time to give them more memories, more moments together before we no longer had any.

A week later, there was a gourd dance out at the Comanche Complex, and I took the boys. Might know, I ran into Clayton Ahtone as soon as I opened the door to Watchetaker Hall. Ever and Quinton scurried under me and through the door. Before I got myself inside, Clayton strolled straight up to me, shook my hand like it was a gourd rattle, and asked, "What tree stump have you been hiding in?"

Ever and Quinton looked up at the two of us like we were a pair of old rugged guys. After a quick introduction, Clayton leaned down and asked the boys, "Did you know me and your grandpa chased tornadoes?"

Quinton's eyes grew big and wide, while Ever scowled and looked away.

"That's right," Clayton said. "When we got back from the war, the civil service hired us to chase tornadoes around Lawton. One came down on us so fast we barely had time to radio back to the Lawton police station. Me and your grandpa jumped into a ditch and prayed Sayn'day would make the tornado go around us. Sure enough, he did. Back then the police drove through town with their sirens blaring and warned people to take cover. We lost a couple police officers in those days. Living in Tornado Alley has its consequences."

I quickly remembered why Clayton was always asked to MC the powwows and gourd dances. He was one of those who never stopped talking. Before he made it to his next breath, he told me, "They're finishing supper break. There's still some food left. Go feed these boys."

I led Ever and Quinton to a series of long tables placed next to each other. They were lined at the back of the building. We picked up plastic plates on one end of a table and made our way down a line of Crock-Pots and food trays. The boys piled their plates high with goulash, mashed potatoes, corn, green beans, and a big piece of fry bread each. We found some empty folding chairs at the back of the arena. Those little guys had twice the food, and ate twice as fast, too. I told them, "Gaa, people are going to think I don't feed you."

Shortly after we threw our empty plates into a large metal trashcan, the powwow singers made their way to the drum and the gourd dancers came to the front of the seating area.

"You see the big sash across that one's chest," I said, and they nodded as we looked at one of the dancers. "The front part of the sash is red and that means he's Kiowa."

"That's his tribe," Ever said.

"Like us," Quinton added.

All the dancers wore nice dress slacks, and either a nice button-down or a ribbon shirt. They had a sash draped around their necks where one side showed the color red and the other side showed navy blue. If the dancer wore the red falling down the left side of their body, it would signify they were Kiowa, and navy blue on the left side meant those dancers were Comanche. I explained to them how all this came from early peyote meetings, and then the formation of the Native American Church. Kiowas started arriving at those meetings wearing red sashes and then Comanches followed suit by wearing blue. Soon this transferred over to gourd dances.

One of the women dancers walked by wearing a series of oak-leaf patterns on her buckskin dress. The left half of the oak leaf was beaded red, while the right was beaded blue. I was excited to tell the boys, "Oak-leaf patterns are Kiowa. See how it's half red and half blue."

The lady noticed us admiring her buckskin dress, so she waved at the boys and smiled. Quinton returned a cheesy smile, while Ever yelled, "You're a Kiowa!" and pointed at her face. The lady's smile faded quickly and she turned away.

"Don't do that, Ever," I said, and pushed his hand back down to his side. "That's rude."

Clayton Ahtone's voice came over the loud speaker, "Vincent Geimasauddle, will you please step into the arena?"

"Did Clayton call my name?" I said out loud. I knew he called my name, but it caught me by surprise.

"As a member of the Black Leggings Society," Clayton

continued, "I would like to honor Vincent and his service to our country."

"Did somebody say your name, Grandpa?" Ever asked.

Quinton yelled, "Did you win?"

I took the boys by the hands and walked them into the arena. We walked around the drum and singers and I made my way to the front, where Clayton stood at a table with the microphone equipment. I didn't have a gourd or any regalia. We were in our street clothes. Mostly, I wanted to show the boys a gourd dance and try my best to explain the traditions to them. How did I end up in the middle of the arena? Once we came to stand between the front tables and the drum, I turned the boys to face the drum, so our backs were to Clayton.

"Vincent was stationed in Japan at the outbreak of the Korean War," Clayton said. "And he was among the first American soldiers to enter combat on Korean soil. Please come out and honor this American war hero."

The lead singer lifted his stick high in the air and came down hard on the drum. The other drummers followed the beat by the second stroke. His voice rose up and started the honor song, and the other singers also fell into a rhythm with the song.

Ever yanked on my hand and asked, "Why is everybody watching us?"

This wasn't a large powwow by any means. The gourd dance portion of the powwow always brought out fewer people than the later portion, when the contests started. There may have been a couple hundred people in the building. Many of them were family of the gourd dancers and some were there for the later part of the powwow—after grand entry—but they mainly came to eat supper. Watchetaker Hall was about half filled. People sat around the arena, walked from place to place, or cleaned tables and took down the food from supper break.

I started to bob up and down with the drumbeat, staying in one spot. Ever and Quinton mimicked what I was doing. Soon all three of us were bobbing up and down at the knees and in rhythm with the drum.

Clayton came from behind us holding three rattles. He shook my hand, handed me a rattle, and then dropped dollar bills at my feet, then did the same with each of the boys. He had his own rattle and began dancing.

I shook my gourd to the drumbeat and the cadence of the song. I noticed Ever and Quinton looking up at me as they mimicked what I was doing. They shook the rattle, making the beads inside *shhhhoooo shhhhoooo* just as the drummers hit the hide on the drum. Soon they were in the same rhythm as my rattle: *shhhhoooo shhhhoooo*. I mimicked the drum with my dance and rattle, and boys mimicked me: *shhhhoooo shhhhoooo*.

Each gourd dancer came to stand in front of me, shook my hand, dropped crumpled dollar bills at my feet, and then moved over to do the same with the boys. Ever and Quinton politely stared at the men as they shook their hands. All the dancers stood to my left and we danced in unison. Twenty men in a line. The women did the same, only they wore shawls instead of carrying gourds, and the women formed a line behind the men. Soon people rose out of their seats and made their way toward us. Two rows of dancers stood with me and my grandsons. We all bobbed up and down to the drumbeat. A few of the women called out with their rolling *lulus*, and a couple of the men sent sharp whoops into the air.

I kept glancing down at my grandsons. Ever's curly hair was a sharp contrast to his cousin's long, straight hair. But the two boys moved exactly the same. They had the same posture and concentrated to the rhythm with the same intensity. Their tiny hands barely held on to the large rattles they were carrying. Up and down they bobbed.

I didn't have to explain any part of the dance to them. They watched me and the other men and mimicked us. I was amazed at how quickly they followed in my footsteps.

And then it scared me.

TURTLE JUGGLED SO much between work, the kids, and Everardo's dialysis treatments—she even took extra hours at TG&Y to make up for Everardo not being able to work—so I hated to ask, but I wanted to learn how to make gourd dance regalia for the boys. Somehow I brought up the topic. Next thing, she pulled into my driveway on a Saturday afternoon.

I rushed outside and said, "Is everybody okay?"

Ever was the first to jump out of Turtle's car, and then Quinton followed. They had brown paper bags in their arms. Quinton said, "These aren't groceries, Grandpa," and Ever said, "Mom took us to an Indian store."

We all made our way into my bedroom. I wasn't so reluctant to have people in my room now, I was four months sober. The boys placed the bags onto the edge of my bed. Then they hopped atop and sat cross-legged, waiting for me to pull items out.

Turtle stood next to me. "I found a few things for you at Eric's Indian Store in Apache."

I pulled out two rolls of red cloth and two rolls of navy-blue cloth. There was a package of white thread and a pack of needles. I pulled out hanks of size eleven seed beads. Reds and blues, but there were oranges and yellows, too. There must have been at least twenty hanks of beads spread across the edge of my bed. The boys kept reaching over to run their fingers down the smooth length of the strands.

Ever said, "I like the sparkly ones."

"I like the ones that look like water," Quinton added.

There was also a pair of scissors, a ruler, measuring tape, pin cushions, and a pattern for a vest.

"The size chart is for men," Turtle said, "but you can take measurements of the boys to make their size."

All the regalia pieces were spread across one end of my bed. The boys sat on the other end. We all stared for a moment. No one said anything—not even the boys. Maybe she wanted to do something because I had been watching the boys during all this mess with Everardo. I must have become a little emotional. Turtle mistook those emotions and told me, "I'll help you learn." Sure I wanted to know how to make all the regalia, but my emotions had more to do with Turtle's generosity. Or maybe more about the boys, having the material to make them something special, unique—that might outlive all of us. I just couldn't bring myself to say. I didn't have the words to fully explain my emotions. But it was something I felt deep inside.

Turtle pulled out the vest pattern and showed me how to measure the boys. She unrolled the measuring tape and placed it against Ever's back. Then she showed me how to adjust the measurements for him. Turtle had always been good with math. It was something that skipped generations, I think. My grandmother was a lot like Turtle, not only in her look, but in her demeanor. And her mind was mathematical in the same way.

"Let me show you one of our family patterns," I told the boys. I ran to the kitchen to grab a pen and paper. "I'm going to put these patterns on the back of your vests."

I drew two triangles atop each other, with the pointed ends touching. It looked almost like an hourglass shape. Then around the triangles I drew a large, four-pointed star. The triangles were the centerpieces to the four points. I told them, "See this pattern. Only our family can wear it. It was handed down to me from my mother's father, Harry Hokeah, who said his mother-in-law, Gapkaugo, dreamed the pattern for him."

"What if I see someone wearing it?" Quinton asked.

"Then punch him in the face," Ever said.

"You're not supposed to hit," Turtle told the boys.

"That's what my teacher keeps telling me."

"But he still does it," Quinton said.

Ever reared back and punched Quinton in the shoulder, yelling, "Shut up!"

Quinton punched him back and yelled, "You shut up!"

Ever jumped on top of Quinton and the two boys rolled off the bed, landing on the floor with a loud thud.

Turtle barked at them to cut it out. I laughed. Once she got the boys to calm down, I explained to them the importance of family emblems and patterns. "They remind us of our ancestors," I told them. "When we pray, we need to know each ancestor by name. These patterns are a record of our family history." The crossing triangles inside a four-pointed star represented a gateway between suns, like a portal between worlds. But it was more than that. It had more to do with traveling, like my mother's maiden name, Hokeah. And if I didn't teach this to my grandsons, then I might be the last one to know.

Before I had the chance to fully explain everything, it was getting late and Turtle needed to take Quinton back to Lila. Sissy also needed to be picked up from her cousin's house. "Thank you, Turtle," I told her. She didn't say anything in return, but just had the boys climb into the car and drove away.

My daughter gave me more than just material items that day. Too, she gave me the power to heal my grandsons. Then I couldn't help but wonder if the meaning ran deeper. Was she healing Ever and Quinton through my hands? The hands that had done so much damage to naw thep'thay'gaw. I stood on my porch and watched Turtle's car disappear down the street. I thought, Was Turtle calling to me the way Kiowas called to our ancestors? Asking for help, but not just material help, a healing help—one that carried through seven generations.

I went back into the house and opened the bottom drawer on my dresser. It was still completely empty. I carefully placed the rolls of cloth next to the hanks of beads, which were stacked beside the scissors, needles, and measuring instruments. Once I had all the items neatly placed inside the drawer, I stared at it for a moment. When I finished organizing a space and it looked new, I always wanted to keep staring. I couldn't help but realize how much power these few items could have. So I kept coming back to the drawer. After I had put on my pajamas, I went back to open it. I stared at the neatly stacked needles and thread and cloth, and then I went to brush my teeth. As soon as I was done brushing my teeth, I came back to my room and opened the drawer again. There the hanks of beads lay next to everything else. I shut the drawer and took my medication, but I had to look in the drawer one more time before I climbed into my bed for the night.

In the next few days, I had the red cloth cut into the shape of small vests. I beaded the touching triangles inside a four-pointed star on the backs of the red cloth. I held them up to the light and admired the cutout of where the arms slid and how even I had cut the lines where the buttons would sit. The vests looked so tiny. It was a different story when I started sewing. I remembered how Turtle told me, "You have to iron the edges, or it'll take you years to finish."

I didn't have years. In fact, I had less than one.

I had been doing so well. I took my diuretics steady and without fail; I knew what I was up against. I didn't dare have any alcohol. I set my watch to an alarm to remind myself to take my medication. Then when I woke up in the night and had climbed out of bed, might know, I suddenly didn't remember why I had gotten up. I looked around my room. It was dark and it felt like I didn't know where I was, but I also knew where I was. It made no sense. "Where was I supposed to go?" I asked myself. Then a warm sensation ran down my leg. I looked down and saw a large wet spot around my crotch. Gaa, even when you're alone in a dark room at night, you can't help but feel real shame. I pulled a change of clothes out of my dresser and cleaned myself. I remembered lying back down in bed that night and all of a sudden couldn't remember having just had the accident. It was like the occurrence was suddenly a dream. Had it really happened? I was too exhausted to stay awake to determine if it had really occurred.

When I woke up the next morning, my mind was clearer, and I knew the accident was real when I found my soiled clothes in the bathroom. But I was too tired to do anything. I kept having moments in the day when I didn't know where I was. Worse still, the confusion hit me fast and faded just as quick. I had no appetite and didn't want to get out of bed. The only reason I pulled myself out of bed was Turtle. I didn't want her to find me out of my mind. She already had enough to worry about with Everardo's dialysis and kidney issues. The last thing she needed was another sick person in her life.

I got dressed and forced myself to crawl inside my truck and drive to the hospital. It didn't take long for them to determine my cirrhosis had progressed. Too, it caused my memory loss. To top it off, I had a blood infection. The doctors hooked me to an IV and started pumping me full of antibiotics. I felt better by the hour. The next morning, I climbed out of my hospital bed and took my IV stand for a walk. One of the nurses saw me strolling around and he tried to get me to lie down.

I told him, "I have regalia to make."

THE NEXT DAY Turtle showed up at my house. "Are you drinking again?"

I told her I wasn't.

"Then why didn't you pick up the boys?"

I had been so sick I had forgotten to call Turtle and Lila to tell them I couldn't get the boys from school. Zadle'bay! I wanted to tell Turtle the truth. Too, I wanted to tell her, "Your dad's dying," and "I'm paying for all those years I was bad to you," but I looked at the ground instead. I couldn't bring myself to burden her with my diagnosis. I couldn't stand the idea of her pitying me when I never gave her the same.

Might know, one screw-up was enough. I had let her down.

Then a month passed without seeing the boys. I missed them. It made me want to drink. Turtle was right to not bring them around anymore. I had messed up. But it was sure lonely without them.

It was a moment of weakness when I decided to drive myself to the drive-up liquor store on Cache Road. I parked in the lot. There was no line at the window. I could've driven up and ordered my usual. One pint of Southern Comfort. But I parked instead. I really didn't want to go up to that window. They would be excited to see me and say something like, "Vincent, you old so and so. Where have you been?" I'd say something playful like, "Oh, living inside that tree stump again." They'd be happy to see me, and say, "Here's a free pint on us," knowing one pint would send me back for more. Then they would have me again. I'd start ordering two pints a night, start stopping by in the middle of the day for extra. I sat in the parking lot and watched as other vehicles pulled up. A brown paper bag would come out of the window. The driver would reach out and grab it. Then another car would drive up and the same thing would happen again. I thought the more I watched customers buy their liquor, the more likely I was to shift my truck into drive and pull up to the window myself. But I didn't. In fact, the opposite happened. The more I watched those cars pull up and leave, pull up and leave, the more I didn't want to go. I kept thinking, Naw thep'thay'gaw—our family. So I made myself stay. I sat in that parking lot for nearly an hour, and I must have watched twenty cars come and go. It was a single memory repeating in my mind: Turtle bringing me the material to make gourd dance regalia. A simple and kind act. Too, she was calling to me, and my ancestors were calling to me. I sat in my truck until I could no longer stand seeing so many customers being handed misery in a bottle. How many families had this one liquor store destroyed?

I drove out of the parking lot and back to my house. I went inside, into my bedroom, and I pulled out the bottom drawer on my dresser. I had completed the vests, which were folded neatly side by side, but I still needed to finish the rattles, belt, and bandolier. I spread everything out in an orderly fashion across the dining room table. I could see what I had and what I didn't have. Soon enough I assessed how to proceed.

The next morning I drove to an antique store and asked them if they had some of the old tin salt and pepper shakers. Back when Kiowas were made prisoners of war and placed in concentration camps, the U.S. government didn't allow us to practice our culture. The only thing we had were government rations called commodities, and in those commodities were tin salt and pepper shakers. Most looked at them and saw salt and pepper shakers, but we looked at them through Kiowa eyes and we saw gourd dance rattles. In secret, out of the military's sight, we practiced our culture, and we modified the rations we had at our disposal. When Kiowas danced with rattles made from tin salt and pepper shakers, it was a proud act of resistance.

I brought home two tin shakers. I punched a hole through the top and bottom of the tin, then I shoved the wooden dowels through the shakers for handles. I pulled out leather and wrapped the bottom of the dowels, where the boys would hold the rattles. I ran streamers of leather from the base. Then I started to bead. One bead at a time—first red and then blue—I stitched the triangles inside the four-pointed star. It took me three days, but I had two rattles when I was done.

I didn't wait for another day to pass before I took the red cloth and cut long and wide strips and did the same with the navy blue. I sewed the two pieces into a narrow sash belt that was half red and half navy blue. The boys would wear the red showing in the front when they danced. I had to go to a hair salon to buy those old-fashioned plastic hair curlers. I wrapped them in cloth and fastened them to the end of the belts, then beaded the family pattern onto them. Then I took red and navy-blue fringe and sewed them onto the end of the belts. Now when the boys tied the belt around their waist, the red would be in front and the red and blue fringe would hang at their sides. My imagination filled with the sight of Ever and Quinton dancing to the beat of our large drums, and the fringe on their sash belts swaying with their motion.

Each day blended into the next, but I kept my focus on making the regalia at my kitchen table. I stopped to eat, but I'd return to my kitchen table soon after and continue with a task that burned hours without me ever noticing.

The mescal beans for the bandolier were the only things that were really a pain to fix. I had to use my drill, which was old but still ran, and I broke two bits in the process of trying to drill holes down the center of the beans. Small, dark reddish brown, and hard as a rock. It took half a day just to drill through enough beans to make beads for the boys' bandoliers, and then I ran red and blue plastic beads in alternating sequence to the mescal beads. They went red, blue, mescal bead and repeated along the three-foot length. It ran in a large loop that would wrap around their bodies. I used a strip of leather to hold the loop together and punched three holes into the leather so as to tie the bandolier. It took me a good while, maybe an hour or so. My old hands didn't have the same strength they once had, so they trembled as I shoved and dug the point of a kitchen knife into the leather.

All told, it took me about a month to make the regalia, and I had been so preoccupied I didn't realize it had been so long since I saw the boys last. I didn't have the energy to clean off the table. Instead, I pushed all the supplies aside and laid out their regalia in the middle to see how it matched. The red vests laid underneath the bandolier. I draped the red and blue sash across the bottom of the vests, where their waists would be, and made sure to face the red side up. Then I sat the gourd rattle on the right side of the vest—for the hand that'd hold it. Kiowa red, with beaded family patterns on each piece. I ran my fingers over the beads, tracing my fingers along the touching triangles and each point of the star. I decided to leave it lying out for the night. I also decided to give Turtle a call, not that she would answer, but I needed to try. When I heard her voice on the other end of the phone, I blurted, "The regalia is done," as fast as I could. I was afraid she would hang up on me.

"Do what?" she asked. "Say it slower."

"I finished the boys' Gourd Dance regalia."

She was silent on the other end. When time had passed a little too long, I asked, "Are you there?"

"Thank you," Turtle told me. "Maybe you should start picking up the boys from school every Friday. That way if there's a dance you can take them."

"I'd like that," I told her.

She told me that Everardo and his brother had been a perfect match for a kidney transplant. He had a new job, too. He was only a part-time car salesman, but it was enough to bring in a little more money. His job was to translate for Spanish-speaking customers at Superior Auto. Sounded like he was "happy guy," with his new job and new kidney. She caught me up on Ever and Quinton and how they kept telling everybody they were Kiowa like their kown. "The color red is for Kiowa," the boys told Turtle, and wanted to make sure she understood. "Sorry but Cherokees don't have a color." We laughed about them. Those boys. They ran me ragged, but I missed them.

It was later that night when things changed quickly. I moaned through the night in my sleep. The only time I moaned at night was when I was getting sick. The next morning my body had completely mutated. My stomach had bloated three times bigger overnight. I tried to get out of bed, but I couldn't stand because my feet were so swollen. My phone was on the kitchen counter. It took me ten minutes to walk fifteen feet. I used the walls and the doors and then the kitchen table and the counter to keep myself upright. I knew I couldn't drive myself to the hospital this time.

The paramedics found me on the kitchen floor. I didn't have any strength and it hurt to walk. It felt like the ambulance took an hour to drive to the hospital. I was relieved to be wheeled into the ER.

My children didn't deserve for me to make them suffer one last time, so I decided to do this on my own. I know I chose alcohol over everyone. But in the end, had I done enough? Can a failed father redeem himself with the hearts of his grandchildren? It made me think of the regalia lying on the kitchen table. In my mind's eye, I saw the two triangles touching at their points, making an hourglass figure inside the center of a four-pointed star. Suddenly, the lines on the beaded triangles started to twist. Stretching and spinning. It was a spiral. It was turning, and it widened. The spiral grew larger and larger, making a tunnel. I wanted to climb out of my hospital bed and walk in. So I did exactly that. And might know, the spiral led me into the center of the sun.

Hayes Shade
(1986)

EVER STOPPED IN front of a mask on the far right wall, gawking. I'd dug bloodroot to dye a face on the gourd, singed horsehair for the curls on its head, carved its crooked nose from a knot in the buckeye wood. The booger masks lining the walls of my store were primarily for the tourists. I'd sold cedar flutes, ribbon shirts, beaded moccasins, and the like, going on twenty years, at Chero-Hawk Indian Store for ten of those years. The locals, Cherokee or not, paid little attention to my traditional masks. Mostly, it was the tourists. But Ever had his eye on one of them as soon as he stepped foot through the door, and he gawked, tell you myself, gawked as though he'd seen a hundred people.

Ever was only ten years old and the grandson to my aunt Lena, my mother's sister. According to Cherokee clan customs, Ever was a nephew, a nephew through a first cousin I hardly knew. Guess that was how relations grew as old got older—more years, more kin. My aunt Lena went and married a Kiowa and spent most of her days living in southern Oklahoma; I never visited, so I'd hardly seen my cousins, much less their kids. Ever, on the other hand, made himself known to me in a peculiar way. Unlike others, I listened to him.

His younger sister was Yolanda, after an aunt on his father's side; except everyone called her Sissy. She was two years younger. Ever took after his mother, Turtle, like a reflection on the water, but he was named after his father. Everyone called his father by his full name, Everardo Francisco Carrillo-Chavez, due to a rumor in his hometown down in Mexico that his father was descended from a Spanish governor.

At Stick Ross Mountain Road, on the outskirts of Tahlequah, right where a bend met Coffee Hallow Road, his family lived in a trailer park—in number two, Ever told me. This was the third place inside a year, he said. I thought, why did they move so many times? Come to find out, his family hid an ugly secret by moving place to place, from Lawton to Duncan, from Duncan 250 miles across Oklahoma to Woodall, and finally here in Tahlequah. I could only imagine how losing a home every few months affected him.

Ever told me how the horn on the school bus made his stomach turn, souring. Sissy, come mornings, was the first one out the front door. Turtle had to shake Ever by the legs to get him up—not that it ever worked. He'd lie under the covers pretending to sleep. After the bus drove away, he would run out the front door and hide in the woods. Turtle learned that it was pointless to search for a child that knew every way to hide in trees, weeds, and shrubs. Her routine was to tell his father before she left for work at the Cherokee Nation convenience store. Ever told me his father cared little about schooling, so he was left on his own.

Soon enough, Ever made himself known to the entire trailer park. One evening, he walked out of the woods and there was a birthday party at trailer six; Sissy played in the yard with a dozen other kids. An old and dying oak tree sat at the back of that trailer park, right where the woods began; it was a roost for chickens. Ever called it the chicken tree. The man that lived in trailer four took his roosters to the cockfights. The chicken tree had around a dozen chickens that bred with those roosters. Ever decided the chickens were disguised witches. He made a sword from a cedar branch and he swung it at the tree again and again, sending leaves into the air; he had these thick curls on his head, and

I can imagine those leaves getting caught in his hair. He riled up those chickens and roosters, making them flap and squawk like a horde of ski-lees.

"Ever!" Sissy yelled from the other side of a fence. The other kids yelled, too, and this was the first any of them knew his name.

"That was awesome," the birthday boy yelled. The words called like a *huh* at the beginning of a stomp song, and shell shakers moved in Ever's chest.

Sissy said, "Come over, Ever." The next set of shells shook in the pit of his stomach.

"I never go by that tree," the birthday boy said. Eventually, his hands joined in the rhythm.

Sissy said, "Nobody will hit us here." The shell shakers shook faster, and that stomp song moved through him like an echo from a hundred years back.

He stabbed his cedar sword into the tip of his toe and dug at his shoe. All those kids stood at the fence, some with red-stained lips, others with frosting on their chins; they all waited for Ever to join the birthday party. After a while, the kids peeled away from the fence to climb onto the trampoline or eat at the table of food. He dug that branch into the tip of his shoe until the rubber tore. Sissy opened her mouth for a final try, hesitated; instead she stopped herself, and ran over to the trampoline. Jumping with her friends, she made an excuse.

"He never wants to play with anybody."

If he knew that trailer six was having a birthday party, he would have wiggled his way underneath the neighbor's barbwire fence, pushed through the thicket of thorns until he made it to the ditch by the dirt road. He would have run through the standing water in the ditch until he came to the back fence around his trailer. He would have thrown himself over that fence and snuck into the trailer completely unseen. Anything to avoid being around other kids.

A WEEK AFTER that birthday party, early morning, he sprinted down the center of the trailer park just after the bus took the other children for school.

Turtle yelled out the front door. "The boogers will snatch you from those woods and cook you for dinner!"

A pile of G.I. Joes lay in the yard of trailer six. These were the birthday boy's presents. Ever climbed the fence, scooped up all the action figures, and hid in the woods. Those G.I. Joes kept him busy and distracted and helped him stay clear of his father and his unpredictable rage.

On the day that a social worker stopped by their trailer, Ever was imagining the boogers his mother warned him about. He imagined them to be mud-covered ski-lees, witches, standing crooked and bent, disguised like an old burnt tree and waiting. Akin to a boogeyman. Ever hid in the bathtub with those stolen G.I. Joes.

Waist deep in water, letting the shower rain down, he sat cross-legged and placed the action figures in different spots around the tub. His father knocked on the door and yelled. With the shower splashing, Ever hardly heard himself playing much less his father yelling. He called back with a loud "Okay." His father muddled a longer sentence. Ever gave him another "Okay," without much notice. His father pounded on the door so hard the frame shook.

"I'm not done yet," Ever called back.

But the door burst open anyway. Ever popped his head around the shower curtain. His father stormed into the bathroom, clutching the knife he had used to unlock the door.

"Get from the water, now," Everardo said. He shut the door behind him. Ever knew the wrinkles in his father's forehead, the thud of his cowboy boots, and the swelling veins on his hands meant that he wanted to grab Ever by the wrist and yank him out of the bathtub. His father aimed a finger at the door, and his hand shook with adrenaline, but also because of the round white pills his father took.

"A social worker out here," his father said.

Quickly, Ever dried himself, as much out of curiosity as fear, because he had no idea what a social worker was. With those action figures cradled in one arm, he stepped into the living room. He didn't bother to look for his mother, Turtle, because she was at work. A young white lady sat on the couch with a notebook and papers in her lap. Everardo sat across from her in the recliner. He said, with his accent getting in the way, "This is him."

"I love your curls," the social worker said, with one of those bright smiles to put him at ease. But Ever turned and went into his bedroom and dumped the G.I. Joes onto his bed. By the time the social worker came into his room, he was on knees and leaning against the mattress.

"I received a call about you. Why aren't you going to school?" She bent down to one knee. She tried to touch his curls, but Ever flinched, so she paused. The social worker explained how some kids "act out" when they are being abused and other kids "close in." Ever didn't know what that meant. She went on to explain about good touch and bad touch. When she asked if his father touched him, Ever blurted out, "No." But when she asked if he hit him, suddenly Ever grew angry and told her to go away. All he wanted to do was set up his action figures.

The social worker took a card from her pocket and laid it on the mattress. She ran her fingers through his wet curls and this time Ever didn't flinch. She looked like she might cry. She hurried down the hallway, and the entire trailer shook when she slammed the front door behind her.

"You make me in jail, stupid," his father said, as he leaned over Ever. On both knees, next to the bed, Ever turned away from the action figures and his father picked up the social worker's card. Ever told me about the wrinkles in his father's forehead and veins popping out on his hands, shaking, and he knew that his father must have wanted to sling him into a wall, or take a thumb tack and stick it into his side. He cringed and waited for his punishment. Instead, his father crumpled the card and disappeared into his bedroom.

Later that evening, Ever and Sissy sat in the backseat of a squad car—alongside Turtle. It was the medication since he lost his kidneys, his mother said, as if Everardo's aggression was explainable. The police officer paid little attention, and he drove them to Tahlequah's battered women's shelter.

THE FIRST TIME Ever stopped at Chero-Hawk, he hid in my store because the kids at the shelter wanted him to play Scrabble. The women's shelter was just twenty yards from my store, so he was bound to wander in my direction. This was when I saw him gawking at a booger mask on the wall for nearly half an hour.

"My brothers and sisters had a meanness that made the devil himself blush," I told Ever that day, doing my best to get his attention. He fidgeted just enough to let me know that he was listening; still he kept his focus on that mask. I called out, "I was teased and harassed by six of them."

Youngest of seven, I had four brothers and two sisters. My family moved into a new home, not necessarily new, but rented, when I was about ten years old myself—all those decades ago. I remembered that house clearly because it was my childhood home. My mother worked hard to keep her seven kids in the same place year after year, and it taught me how to belong—not only to my mother but to my community. We Cherokees followed our lineage through our mothers. When I thought of that house, I always thought of my mother, coming home late after work to throw a mess of food on the stove.

We had a massive locust tree smack in the middle of the front yard. Its seedpods were long and narrow, hanging from branches like snakes or fingers, turning brown then black. Around late fall and early winter a whole mess of these seedpods would lay in the front yard, underneath that locust tree. I didn't want anything to do with a tree that had creepy seedpods reaching down, as if to grab me. And my brothers liked to pelt the seeds at my face; once, they pinned me on the ground and shoved pods into my mouth. My sisters were clever, not brutal, like my brothers. One sister distracted me at the dinner table while the other slipped a seedpod onto my food. I climbed into bed one night, and when I was almost asleep, I brushed my foot across a seedpod. Every time I touched a seedpod I screamed, and I screamed so much and so often that my mother told me I had a high pitch that would make a little girl jealous.

Eventually she had enough. I walked into the kitchen one afternoon to find a bucket full of those locust tree seedpods. I was sure it was the work of my brothers and sisters. I ran into the living room, calling for my mother—ready to tattle, tell, and cry—but there was an old man sitting on the couch. He held this heavy coffee-colored cane at his side. His skin had the texture of a turtle's hide. His jaw seemed to hang lower than normal. My mother was at the store, he told me. He introduced himself as an uncle, a Bird Clan member, someone distant but a relative. He spoke like he had a mouthful of food, slow, almost a mumble, so I nearly misunderstood when he said the bucket of seedpods were his. Come to find out, my mother called on a medicine man to help cure me because I was always aus-guy, what she said was a deep, unnatural fear.

The reason I followed him into the kitchen had to do with how he teetered on the coffee-colored cane as he lifted himself from the couch, the even and deliberate pace when he moved foot-to-cane, foot-to-cane, and how his long jaw gave him a silly smile, wide, broad, with deep creases in his cheeks.

He spilled the seedpods onto the counter. His cane was hooked over the edge of the sink next to him, in case he got dizzy. I stood behind him, beside his shoulder, for the same reason. Not that I would have been able to do much if he did fall, being a child. We both would have ended up with broken hips.

He popped open pods and made a pile of the seeds, and I stood at his side.

As he worked, he told me about booger masks and how there was once a traditional dance where they were worn. I listened out of politeness—my mother would have been upset if I offended an elder relative. He described how dancers snuck out of the woods on a feast day celebration, wearing the booger masks. The dancers scared everyone at the gathering, yelled at them, postured, made threats; it was all done in mocking and primarily for laughter. They pretended to grab the women, pretended to fight the men, who pretended to fight off the dancers. They fled into the woods and swore to return on another day.

In all his years, he had never seen Cherokees do this dance; he called it a forgotten memory and said only a few people made the booger masks anymore.

The old man separated all the seeds from the pods and he told me to go get a grocery bag that he left on the front porch. He reached into the bag and took out this piece of wood carved from a poplar tree. He also took out a small bowl filled with tree sap, which he used like paste. The split pods became big lips. In half, the split pods made for thick eyebrows. His hands were wide, fingers long, skin pale, covered in spots. Even though his hands shook, they moved with strength as he formed the booger mask. He pasted clumps of the seeds together to make round eyeballs. After that, he stuck a row of seeds between the lips to make teeth but left a couple of spaces to give it this crooked smile. Then he cut a pile of pods in half and fastened them to the top of the head, giving the booger mask this spiky hair that stood straight up.

There was something funny when an adult acted like a child. That old man lifted the mask to his face. Maybe it was the way he held the mask off-angle, maybe it was how his wrinkled fingers shook, but I never laughed so hard. A few moments later, my mother pulled into the driveway. I ran outside with that mask in my hands, to show my mother what the old man gave me as a gift. Placing the booger mask against my own face, guess where I stopped and stood: underneath that locust tree, on top of the brown and black seedpods.

"A booger mask helped me overcome a deep fear," I told Ever on the day he stared at one on the wall. I asked him, "Do you have any fears?"

That's when Ever told me about living in the shelter, how it was just down the street from my store, how he hated to be around other kids, but mostly how he had displaced his family.

A FEW DAYS after Ever and I swapped stories, Turtle managed to get him and Sissy out of the women's shelter. An apartment opened up at these low-rent duplexes, Cherokee Village. Turtle had entered a program funded by the state and was paid a stipend every month to attend vocational school, which gave her the money to rent the duplex. She enrolled in the general-office-clerk classes out there at Bill Willis Skill Center, and Ever and Sissy started going to Sequoyah Elementary, right behind my store, here, across the alley.

On his first day at Sequoyah, Turtle put Ever's clothes on the edge of his bed and told him to wake up and get ready for school. Ever lay underneath the covers, not exactly asleep and not exactly awake, either. Turtle came to sit on the edge of his bed. She told him about how things were turning around for the family, how she worked to get them into a new home that would be theirs forever. "I signed up for an Indian Home," she said, and explained how Cherokee Nation distributed homes, a home where he and Sissy would have a front and back yard. They had to wait until their names rotated to the top of the list. It might be a few years, but it was something to look forward to. Things could be different, with nobody around to hit him. But in order to take care of the family, Ever had to go to school; if Turtle had more than three absences, the Skill Center would ask her to leave. She laid a hand on his leg, rubbed his calf, and said, "Please, don't do this, Ever."

He flipped around under the covers and pulled the blanket over his head.

Turtle kicked the side of the bed. She slammed the door. The tires on her car screeched when she pulled out into the street, taking Sissy to school—Ever thought. An hour or so later, Ever sat on the bedroom floor surrounded by G.I. Joes when he heard his mother drive back up to the apartment. A second car parked in the next space over; the engine ran smoother, cleaner, it was a new car, for certain. Two car doors opened and shut. Turtle spoke with someone, a lady, as she climbed the front steps.

Ever tried to ignore the banter in the living room, the

footsteps coming down the hallway. He unscrewed the screws on the backs of his action figures, pulling them all apart. Heads lay in one pile, legs in another, arms stacked together, and a mound of chests.

A white lady, six inches taller than his mother, introduced herself as the school principal, Mrs. Edwards, and extended her hand. From the floor, Ever looked up, cringed at the size of her fingers, and then turned away. All her bright makeup gave her peculiar shadows and plastic-looking skin. She pulled her hand back, straightened herself, and let out a huff.

"Get in the car, you will go to class," Mrs. Edwards said. She bit her lip, squinted, and told him. "Or I will call the police."

The principal and Turtle followed Ever down the front steps. Ever put his backpack in reverse, on his chest, arms underneath the straps. He clutched it tight from the front steps to the backseat, from Cherokee Village to Sequoyah Elementary. When Turtle parked at the rear of the school, across the alley, in that narrow gravel lot, Ever buried his face into the backpack's rough fabric, even deeper once the principal parked alongside.

Voices carried from the rear of the cars, talking, his mother and the principal, initially, and then male voices joined in the conversation. Ever turned around to see out the back window. Three men stood with Turtle and Mrs. Edwards. One was tall and broad, his arms long. Another wore gym clothes—tight shirt and athletic shorts. The other had thick arms that bowed away from his round body.

His mother's car faced the back of my store and the women's shelter, and Ever looked from one to the other, his eyes watering. Chero-Hawk Indian Store and the battered women shelter were more like mirages, from my guess, like the watery spots down a long and straight road. He buried his face, again, into the backpack, the fabric sliding across his forehead, nose, and cheeks, wiping the tears.

The passenger door opened. The front seat buckled forward. Turtle stood outside, and said, "Okay, Ever, you need to go to class."

Mrs. Edwards said, "Guys, let's not drag this out."

The tallest teacher reached into the backseat, grabbed him by the arm. Ever twisted and pulled away. He grabbed Ever again, this time with a better grip, and pulled him halfway out of the backseat. The other two teachers latched onto his jeans and shirt. Ever pressed a foot into the bottom of the folded front seat and locked his leg. One of the teachers yanked against the back of his leg and buckled his knee forward. Ever did the same with his arm, pressed his palm into the back window. His elbow buckled the same as his knee. Before he could grab onto the side of the door, it was shut behind him.

The teachers released him and Ever fell against the side of his mother's car. The backpack still in his arms, he pushed against his tears with his palms. Hands on their hips, heads turned up, the three teachers panted, trying to catch their breaths. Mrs. Edwards stood at the rear of the cars, her arms crossed and folded. Turtle hid her tears by studying the gravel rocks at her feet.

Then Ever darted away from the parked cars, that backpack still in his arms. He sprinted down the alley. Sequoyah Elementary on his left, the women's shelter on his right, he left them all in the gravel parking lot.

He circled back around the block, made his way to Chero-Hawk without anyone noticing. His mother, the principal, and the teachers searched the neighborhood before they came to this strip of stores. I gave him a glass of water, and tissue for his eyes and nose. He had plenty of time to tell me what had happened before his mother stepped through the door to my shop.

You know how you pause when you recognize someone? I must have paused just like that, mouth open and dumbstruck. "Turtle, it's me," I wanted to say, "Your cousin, Hayes Shade." But Turtle looked angry as she grabbed Ever by the hand. This wasn't the time. Also, she didn't seem to recognize me. She just led Ever toward the door.

"Wait," I called, and hurried across the store, nearly knocking over a buffalo headdress. I pulled that booger mask off the wall and handed it to Ever, and said, "This belongs to you."

The last I seen of Ever was his eyes growing wide as he admired his gift. He turned the mask around in his hands, and then came face to face with it. He stared at it like looking into a mirror, as if a distorted version of himself stared back.

Time, like masks, could make us reclaim the best of who we were and purge the worst of what we'd become. Ever faced the mask, faced his fears, and I hoped the mask healed him the way it once healed all Cherokees.

Lila Geimausaddle-Quoetone
(1990)

I COULDN'T BELIEVE my eyes. Ever was so big—stretched tall—like a war staff. The little birdie I remembered had grown into a kutho'heen. It was at a convenience store over in Anadarko. I pulled into the parking lot and saw a scary guy pacing back and forth, and then he slammed his fist into the side of a pay phone. I hit my brakes—looked around—hoping for other people. Only if it wasn't so late at night. I looked a little harder at the man's face, but he wasn't a man at all, just built like one. It was Ever. His almond eyes and downward-curving lips like his grandfather's. I quickly parked my car and jumped out, and I reached out to give him a hug. Gkoi way, he was more of a son than a nephew.

"My ta'li," I said. "What happened to you? Why are you so mad?"

My sister, Turtle, had called me that night. "Ever is on the streets of 'Darko. Lila, can you pick him up?"

I was in Lawton. She was in Tahlequah. I'd reach him before her and it was late. Turtle was a four-hour drive away. It'd take me forty-five minutes. How did he end up in 'Darko? Turtle told me Ever kept asking to go to his father's house in Lawton. Then after months and months, she had to stop saying no. At first, I thought maybe it had something to do with Everardo's health. She always felt sorry for his father. Since Everardo's kidneys had failed ten years before, he hadn't been the same since. And to think his own brother gave him one of his kidneys—real waste. Ever must've been in kindergarten back then. But he was ten years old the last time he saw his father. Now he was almost fifteen—stretched tall—the way teens do. The more he grew, the more mon'sape, like when Sun Boy didn't listen to Grandmother Spider, so to speak. Turtle told me about the holes in his bedroom walls. He had been expelled from school for breaking a kid's nose. She grew scared of her own son. Sending him to visit his father was an act of desperation.

THE VISIT STARTED a little awkward because it was almost like Ever was meeting his father for the first time. So much was different and unfamiliar. Like his father's house, which wasn't much of a house, more of a shed. Everardo was small, too—five foot three at best. I imagine he weighed one twenty, maybe one thirty in those bright cowboy boots. His house had a living room–slash-bedroom, an almost-bathroom, and a narrow kitchen no bigger than most closets. His disability checks barely paid the rent. There was a single rickety dresser to one side of the living room, just in front of a twin-sized bed and across the room from a tattered love seat. His father kept his old button-down cowboy shirts in the top drawer of that scratched dresser; two pairs of cowboy boots sat on the floor at the base. His father always wore sunglasses—redness in his eyes, scraping from cataract removal. His skin was splotchy with large pores because of the medications he took for failed kidneys.

"You want to go with me?" Everardo asked with one of those thick Qop'thawkoi accents. He left the *t* off "want" and replaced *th* with an *s*.

Ever simply nodded.

He had been at his father's house in Lawton maybe an hour. Then Everardo drove him out of Lawton and headed east toward Duncan. The stretch of road between Lawton and Duncan ran so straight for so long with so much of nothing, it was like time stopped altogether. I called it Southern Plains Hypnosis. The plains appeared like an ocean to the north of the road, and wind pushed grass in waves up to the edges of the highway. There was a fork in the road just before Duncan, and Everardo took the fork north toward Chickasha. He drove Ever through Chickasha—over to 'Darko—then south toward Apache. They must have been on the road a few hours and Everardo didn't say a word. Likewise, Ever didn't say a word back. His first day with his father was spent in hours of silence and driving.

In Apache, they stopped at Red's Café. It was one of those old diners that hangs on to life well after its prime. It had large windows facing the street. There was chipped white paint on the cement walls. I always avoided it. If I had to stop for food in Apache, I usually stopped at the Mazzio's Pizza across the street.

The first thing Ever noticed was that he and his father were the only dark-skinned people in the restaurant. Ever nervously glanced around—avoided eye contact—glares from the thaw'koi. For some reason, Everardo didn't appear to notice the dirty looks. Everardo smiled at the waitress when she asked him what they wanted from the menu. After he said stirred eggs, flat potatoes, and the hard bread, he ended his sentence with "alrighty." Sent the waitress a big smile. She couldn't help but smile back. People always melted. As long as I'd known Everardo, since he started dating my sister back in the early seventies, he'd play with an Okie twang through his Mexican accent, rolling out words like "alrighty" and "reckon" and "you'uns" to mix with phrases like "do what?" and "suppose so" and "figured as much." In that instant, the waitress relaxed her shoulders and asked them how their day was going.

"Just fine," Everardo said, and told the waitress about their drive along the state highways. "The row of wind is longer than a moth on Mondays," he said.

The waitress paused—threw her head back—laughed deep and hard. Other customers turned to watch. She said, "You mean, 'the road is longer than a month of Sundays.'"

"Yes," Everardo said.

She reached over and ran her hand alongside the stubble on his cheek, saying "You're silly."

From the first time he heard an Oklahoman banjo out a phrase, he was always fascinated with the strange accent. He'd change up sayings, like "Turn me upside down and start me a-grinning" with "Turn me into a clown and start from the beginning." He smiled when others laughed at him. It wasn't so much enunciating it correctly. He enjoyed the genuine attempts and genuine failures. Everardo smiled at the food when it came out, smiled with a toothpick in his mouth after the meal, and didn't say a single word to Ever the entire time. After eating at Red's Café, they continued south out of Apache and drove back to Lawton.

EACH MORNING, EVER rolled over in the love seat as his father walked out the front door to go drink coffee at a neighbor's house. One morning, a couple days after Ever arrived, he came back from his morning coffee with three books. His eyes were wide and excited as he woke Ever from his sleep.

"Look," Everardo said, "My friend have this. I take it for you."

Ever sat up onto the edge of the love seat. He reached out for the books, shuffled them between his hands. All were a part of a Western series called *The Spanish Bit Saga*, by Don Coldsmith. The first book was titled *Trail of the Spanish Bit*, followed by *The Elk-Dog Heritage*, and lastly *Follow the Wind*.

"See," Everardo said, and pointed to the image on the first book. It was a Spaniard dressed in a buffalo hide, holding a spear, and with a feather hanging in his hair.

Ever turned the books over in his hands, examining them for their contents. He didn't know that Spanish and In'din people had married back then. Ever only knew about Mexican and In'dins like him today. There was only one other family member who married a Qop'thawgkoi, like his mother had, and Ever didn't associate with that side of the family very often. The only other Mexican Indian he interacted with was his younger sister. He spent the next days with those books, like looking into muddy water for his own reflection, and he learned the Spanish brought in their horses. He thought of how the Kiowa emblem depicted an image of a Kiowa on horseback. It was the horse that allowed Native people to populate the plains.

Too, the Kiowa wore tribal symbols in clothing, like a red cape from a Spanish officer. And Kiowas wore the color red to traditional gourd dances and peyote meetings. The more he explored Spanish culture, the more he realized it intertwined with Kiowa culture, and the more he wanted to learn. It was the first time he really gave any thought to the history of the two groups of people who gave him the blood running through his body, how they'd been intermarrying for hundreds of years.

The first few weeks with his father were spent sitting on the love seat reading and rereading those same three books. His father sat on his bed and watched shows on an old twelve-inch box television set. Once a day, his father sent him up the road to buy freshly sliced deli cuts. It was an old mom-and-pop store, the type no one sees anymore. Every day, Ever slapped on headphones—walked up the road— listened to rap tapes. His father's neighborhood was typical as far as neighborhoods go in Lawton, old houses with faded and chipped white paint. Every street looked the same. He always bought the peppered salami and slices of cheese from blocks sitting inside coolers. He carried home the food and ate the meat quick. Ever was fourteen—growing fast—like teens do. He was already five seven at the time and weighed nearly a hundred and fifty pounds. Food never lasted.

One day his father asked him if he wanted to go to a quinceañera for a cousin. "Araceli," he told him, but Ever couldn't remember her and didn't recognize the name. Still, he agreed—drove out of Lawton—headed north toward 'Darko. The quinceañera was held inside a building that was part of a strip mall.

"I don't speak any Spanish," he told his father.

"It doesn't matter," Everardo said. "You don't have to. Just stand there."

Ever refused to go inside. He heard the Spanish music vibrate through the walls. He nervously watched as dozens upon dozens of Mexican people filtered into the building, half of which were his family. He slid on his headphones, hit play on his tape player, and turned up the volume. Drowned out the music coming from the building. A half hour later, Everardo came back outside.

"You need to go inside. You aunties in there. You cousins in there. They tell you hello. Now go inside."

Ever shook his head and stayed planted in the passenger seat of his father's car.

"Remember, you and Araceli play together?" Ever shook his head. His father barked at him in Spanish—walked back into the building—slammed the door behind him.

A few minutes later, his father walked back out. Ever thought his father would harass him again. Instead he had someone with him—a younger lady, around Ever's age. Her dark blond hair was feathered and she wore a big white dress with intricate silver designs. Ever rolled down the window on the car because he didn't want to open the door.

The young lady walked up to the open window with a plate of food in her hands.

"Hi, Ever. I'm your cousin, Araceli."

"Hey," Ever said.

"My mom wanted me to bring you some food. Are you hungry?"

Ever nodded.

Araceli handed him the plate of food, and said, "Come inside when you're done. Everybody is excited to see you. We haven't seen you in a long time."

Ever took the food from Araceli, said, "Okay," but waited for her to walk away.

He tore into the tamales—scarfed down enchiladas—like a mighty kutho'heen, so to speak. He told me how he used pieces of fresh tortilla to scoop up the beans, like he did with fry bread. His father stood outside the car for less than a minute—real quick—and Ever wiped out that food. When he handed his father the empty plate, he felt nauseous and tried to hold a hand over his mouth. He barely had enough time to jump out of the car before he vomited everything back up. It spread on the ground between his father's car and the car alongside.

"Why you do this?" his father yelled, and barked, "Ni modo!" before storming back into the building. Ever kept vomiting until all the food was out of his stomach.

Feeling sick, he climbed into the car and let his head lay

back on the seat—closed his eyes for a while. He opened them a few minutes later. He looked through the windows of the building and saw his father sitting at a table. A beer in his hands—taking drinks—laughing. One of Everardo's cousins or friends, somebody, stepped up to him and handed him a shot of whiskey. His father knocked back the alcohol without hesitation. Ever watched his father drink beer after beer, round after round, and Ever grew angrier and angrier each time. His father became more animated. He talked to everyone around him. He made people laugh so easily. More and more people gathered nearby. His father quickly became the center of attention. Then his father grabbed some woman and pulled her into his lap with an arm around her waist. She laughed and took a drink of his beer. Everardo leaned in and kissed the back of the lady's neck.

Ever turned away, opened the car door, and jumped out. He slammed the door shut and punched the window. He paced back and forth for a few seconds and then saw a half-broken cinder block laying near a dumpster. He picked up the cinder block and carried it back to his father's car. Ever lifted the stone into the air—two hands—then smashed it into the driver's side window. The glass shattered with a loud boom! But it wasn't louder than the Mexican folk music blasting from the building. Ever looked into the building's window again, and saw his father kissing the lady full on the lips. He turned away and ran into the streets of 'Darko, to the convenience store.

He called his mother collect from a pay phone, and Turtle called me. She said he was at the convenience store by McDonald's. Anadarko was a small town. It only had one McDonald's. I'm sure when I arrived to pick up Ever forty-five minutes later the quinceañera was still going, and Everardo was somewhere inside the building getting drunk with a beautiful woman. Ever was so angry. I got an earful on the drive back to Lawton. He was too mad and too young to really understand. But we'd grown up with an alcoholic father. Everardo had all he could handle—he'd given up.

"Ni modo," he'd told Ever. I'd witnessed the same defeat from my father. Everardo was on his way to drinking himself to death, hiding his failure inside empty beer bottles.

We only hoped to keep Ever from doing the same.

Quinton Quoetone
(1993)

GAA, WE WERE just little guys, around a year old, when Kiowas started getting that ahon'giah back in '76, no, maybe in '77. It was the coalition of Kiowas, Comanches, and Apaches that leased a tract of land to Fort Sill military base for one hundred years. Good thing, too, because us Kiowas divided our share of the money between all tribal members, fifteen hundred a piece. Those of us under the age of eighteen had our money held in trust, growing interest until our day. We were the last in our families to hear our mothers say, "Your per cap check is on the table."

My birthday landed two months before yours. On your

day, you burst into a laughing fit, and I told you, "Ever, calm yourself down, guy." On my day? I simply said, "Your boy, Quinton, just got paid," and I maintained all the way into the bedroom. But we both tore into those envelopes faster than the last meat pie on a plate—ripped out those stiff government checks, too. Remember the Statue of Liberty imprint in the upper left corner? Remember the line of numbers in the center right? Mine was $9,826. 17. The hot-off-the-press scent from that crisp paper hit us like the cool wall of air when we walked into the Bank of Oklahoma.

Might know, the lady behind the counter did the same to you as she did to me. She glanced from the check to our face and back to the check again, tapping those red plastic fingernails on the counter. Her eyes barely squinted when she asked us how we managed to get our hands on that kind of money. You told her the tribe wanted us to help neglected bank tellers buy bleach for untreated roots. I had a permanent grin that no one would spoil, so I asked her if she dated Kiowas and she said no, so I asked her if she dated Comanches and she said no, so I asked her if she dated Cherokees and she said no. Gaa, guess I was out of luck because I was all out of tribes. We waved at the bank teller as we pushed open the doors—that ma'bane pretended not to notice; still, even she couldn't ignore the six thousand in the checking account or the four thousand in our pockets.

Wasn't it our oldest cousin, Leanne, who put her entire per cap in savings? Or maybe it was her sister, Bessie? They saved the money for books and tuition at the University of Oklahoma. We had been dreaming about spending that ahon'giah for three years, since our boy Black Tail's older brother, Big Bow, got his per cap. He cruised into the south side of Lawton, our section of the city, the View, in a Cadillac Seville. That Cadillac was new-used, uptown, clean enough to pass for brand-new. Stink, guy, too, as he bumped down Eleventh Street and turned into the Convenience Store on three-wheel motion. Right then, that's when we knew we were not like Leanne and Bessie.

On my day, my dad warned me, "Quinton, fast money goes fast," and he drove us to OKC where I could find a good car cheap. It took us an hour—hour and a half—to drive up I-44, and I flashed open the bank envelope a dozen times, showing you and Dad both how the hundreds lined up as smooth as beads down a loom. On your day, I drove you to OKC myself. We were going to turn money into a line of colognes, hundreds, fifties, and twenties bottled and packaged.

Your Monte Carlo sat middle row front at Honest Harry's dealership. You grabbed my arm so tight I lost circulation, said, "Quinton, pull over," six times. That dealer was bull-headed about the three-thousand-dollar price written on the windshield. What about twenty-five hundred, cash? He took the fresh bills, bulldogged, and signed over the title to your Monte. My Cadillac El Dorado dripped clean from a fresh car wash, gleamed gold with that tan paint job in the bright sunlight; it faced the main office at Classy Cars. The dealer wanted to take it home until I flashed open that bank envelope. He took four thousand, easy, didn't even have to haggle for my El Dog.

Once back in Lawton, you still had cash in your pocket after buying your car, but on my day I had to stop by the Bank of Oklahoma again. That same teller said I had to wait three days for a check to clear. Why did she give me four thousand the day before? I asked to see the manager. "Oh, it was a *government* check," that ma'bane told me. She flipped her long hair to the other side of her face and pulled two thousand from the drawer.

At Sound Wave, it cost me some serious cash for those twelve-inch speakers, that four-hundred-watt amp, a noise reducer, and an equalizer. My bass was clean and low, but I only had enough money left over for gas and McDonald's. You liked your music hard and dirty, so you dropped the last of that fifteen hundred for some eighteens inside a plexiglass box.

Low on funds, we weaved through the back roads of Lawton and returned to the Bank of Oklahoma. Was it on your per cap or mine when we ran to the building one minute before closing? That teller was already locking the doors. She gave us a smirk, spun on her heels, and disappeared into the bank. We cruised away blasting the latest tape by the Zotigh Singers and shook the building with waves of intertribal beats. We hit the back roads, again, crept into the View, and parked on Black Tail's front lawn. That intertribal wave carried with the same rumble of those artillery shells from the practice rounds at Fort Sill—the ones that shook the entire city of Lawton; proud guys, we danced the way Kiowas danced, and reminisced about per caps gone by.

It was funny how our boy Mike's older brother, Awthaw, went down to Dallas, Texas, bought an old school T-Bird, and tricked it out with the blue and silver colors of the Dallas Cowboys football team. After partying for a week in a motel, he went to a Cowboys football game a'daw, drunk'daw, and lost the last of his per cap in the stands. Uncle Hank had to Western-Union him money so he could get back to Lawton. Everyone teased him that some goofy, rugged guy probably ripped him off.

Even worse, too, was our cousin, Lawrence, from Gotebo. Mr. All-Day-A'daw. He bought that dually truck, slapped on a new set of mud-bogging tires, and took his little crew up to Tahlequah for Cherokee National Holiday. He danced at the powwow and then watched the bronc riders at the rodeo. On the last day, he woke up in a field face-down in a wet cow patty. The first thing he said was "Buh," and a clump of patty fell out of his mouth.

On your per cap and mine both, Uncle Ears staggered up to the back of our cars, slapped the trunk, and said, "Giddyup!" A can of Schlitz in his hand, he lifted the beer in the air, stumbled with the change of wind. We told him,

"Stagger straight, guy." He dropped his beer, forgot about it by the time it hit the ground, left it there spilling, too, and asked, "When's the per cap party, pobs?"

We called our cousin, Jesse, because he was a Munoz Kiowa, and that Munoz side of the family had all the killer weed hookups. He said we could get a pound of Mex for five Cs or a half pound of Salmon River for ten, and if we really wanted some ill weed we could put down twelve Cs for a quarter pound of that Purple Kush. He asked us if we wanted a little crank or some coke and maybe a few rocks. We said yes to the crank, maybe to the coke, but we passed on the rocks. "Do you have the loot for all this?" he asked us. Guess who's got per cap? Since Ears was right there, we asked him to buy liquor for us, and he said, "Sure thing, pobs." We made a list: A fifth of Black Label JD, a liter of Canadian Mist, a liter of Seagram's Seven, Cisco and Boone's for the ladies, and we could not forget about all that Southern Comfort, four liters, two pints, and one half-pint for good luck.

We invited those Ahhaitty girls because they were hard-core and fine as hell. Since you were tight with the Stopps you called them Cherokees from Tahlequah, and those Stopp boys called the Kingfishers and the Phillips and the Shades. I called the Tapptos and the Chasenuhs. We let the Tahsequahs know, so they passed the word to the Burgess family. Ears told all the Quoetones and Geimausaddles in Lawton. We ran into a Hokeah walking out of a bookstore in the mall and he rambled about his bag full of someone named Momaday. You said, "No way, he might bring that bag of books to the party."

We sat in the parking lot of the bank so early the next morning that we watched the tellers climb out of their cars. Little Miss Ma'bane didn't see us as she walked across the parking lot like a constipated chicken in her too-tight skirt and jacket. She opened the doors five minutes late, because we stood waiting outside. You gave her that squint and roll with your eyes. I had that grin and wink. Again, she acted like she was wiping dirt off her hands when she handed us money.

It was your per cap when Jesse met us at Black Tail's house, right? No, wait, it was mine, because I paid out fifteen hundred for a half pound of Salmon River and a few eightballs of crank; he had that supply in his trunk. You wanted a duffle of that ill weed, a taste of crank, and an eightball of coke; he had to track down his supplier, so we met him outside that strip club Sidewinders. You spent thirty-five hundred that day. As we pulled away from the drive-up liquor store on Cache Road, Uncle Ears called the glass bottles in the brown paper bag "forty-niner wind chimes." The clanking glass rang out as we sped through the streets of Lawton.

On two different days, two months apart, but, damn, we did it almost the same way. We paid for two double rooms at that Motel 6 on Lee Boulevard. You walked through the rooms and had to light a few sticks of incense. I smoked a bowl so the rooms would have that fresh-from-the-field smell. By ten o'clock we had people leaning on the walls, lying on the beds, and sitting on the dressers; those double rooms were packed like the tobacco at the end of our cigarettes. Quarters bounced into the air and clinked against the edges of shot glasses, cards slid between fingers and across the tops of televisions, while dominoes clacked over the wood floors.

At my per cap party, everyone called me "Quinton the Mon'sape." I took in too much bud too soon and chilled out too quick, so I snorted a few bumps to pick me up. I shouldn't have popped a chunk of crank or maybe I shouldn't have drunk SoCo straight from the bottle for an hour. I needed to drain the pipe, but all the bathrooms were full, so I went out into the parking lot. That was when I blacked out. You said you found my jeans and shirt next to my El Dog. Then you found my socks and underwear on the sidewalk. The motel manager saw me running down Lee Boulevard naked with my shoes draped around my neck. You found me at the drive-up window outside KFC, trying to trade my shoes for a box of barbecue chicken wings. You, Mike, and Black Tail had to tackle me in the parking lot and drag me into my El Dog. We sped down Lee Boulevard with police sirens somewhere in the distance. You said I was laughing the whole time, too. I was buck-naked guy and refused to put my clothes back on.

But, you, at your per cap party. Bay'gaw! I tried to tell you, "Ever, calm down," even told you to put away the coke. When you hit that line of crank, gulped the Mist, and screamed so loud everyone in the motel room paused: Gaa, I just knew. You ran up and down the room, yelling about being a killer. Some kind of killer, slipping on spilled liquor and falling headfirst into the corner of the television. Me and Black Tail lifted you off the floor and you had a big bump right in the middle of your forehead. Guess the killer grew a horn. We carried you outside and you passed out in the front seat of your Monte. Next thing, a loud crash came from the parking lot. Everyone rushed through the door or pushed back the curtain on the window. Your Monte had all its windows busted out and all the tires were flat. You had some dude pinned against the trunk of a car, working over his face. Mike and Black Tail pulled you off. I laughed. Turned out, that dude mistook your Monte for someone else's. He didn't expect someone to be passed out in the front seat. Your horn grew three inches that night after seeing your Monte all jacked up.

Gaa, we were tearing it for the tribe.

The next day I walked into my house and my head thumped like the lowriders cruising through the View. My mother said that her beading sales were down for the past couple months and she wasn't sure if she could make the rent-to-own payment on her washer and dryer set. Her car was acting up so she asked me if I could go to the commodity building in Carnegie and get food for the month. "If you have the gas money," she told me. Your mother sat in a pow-wow chair in your living room, rubbing her feet because her work shoes had worn out. She told you, "Paying the bills makes your body ache." After seven years on Cherokee Nation's waiting list, you guys had finally gotten your Indian Home. The only thing, though, you were sleeping on pallets of blankets and sitting in powwow chairs for six months.

We took our final trip to the Bank of Oklahoma. This time ma'bane was happy to hand us the last of our per cap money. She even circled the remaining balance with a red pen. The number was different on your receipt, only by pennies. It read something like $6.17. We shoved the last eighteen hundred in our pockets. I kept my receipt in an empty speaker box, with a motel room key, car title, and a signed liquor bottle. You wadded up the receipt and rolled it across the counter; it fell to the teller's feet.

I went to the grocery store and packed two carts with food. I wanted one month without commodities. I paid off my mother's washer and dryer set, and might know she rented-to-own a new television. I bought out the entire stock of size-eleven seed beads at Eric's Indian Store in Apache. She had hanks of beads spread across her beading table and it was the first time she hugged me so tight. I found that huge black-and-white photo of Chief Satanta over in 'Darko; it was in the gift shop at the Southern Plains Indian Museum. For my mother, I used the last eighty dollars in my pocket.

You paid on the house for that month. You told your mom, "All those years ago you lost your first house, and now you don't have to worry anymore. I'm going to fill it with furniture." You went to a used furniture store and bought three full-sized beds, a couch and love seat set, and a dining table. At Wal-Mart, you found three pairs of your mother's favorite work shoes. She lined all three pairs next to the front door and kept glancing over, said, "Happy birthday," every time. You surprised her at that ICOT annual pow-wow in Tulsa by giving her your last one hundred dollars. She had fresh cans of Pepsi all evening. She bought two dozen raffle tickets for the fifty-fifty pot and just as many raffle tickets for a similar black-and-white photo of Chief Satanta. She lost the fifty-fifty, but she nearly tripped over herself hurrying into the arena when she won that photo.

Our mothers echoed words they had echoed before—this time we listened. "Being Kiowa will forever be about how we dance together." Seemed like, being sisters, those words were a song that made them family, but more important: it made all Kiowas come together.

Since we were descendants, our mothers framed those photos of Chief Satanta. He sat on the edge of a log, a bow and arrow held across his lap, in a pose that said: I know how to use these weapons. My mother bragged, "Quinton has his handsome eyes and soft brow line." Your mother said, "Ever has his strong jaw and downward curving lips." Chief Satanta had endured the genocide and still held Kiowas together. His strength flowed through all of us and continued to pull Kiowas close to family and community. *Gaa*, those same black-and-white photos still hang in the middle of our mothers' living room walls, too.

Turtle Geimausaddle

(1995)

NEAR SIX MONTHS ago, maybe seven, I stopped at the video section in Reasor's grocery store and searched rows of movies, where I spied a pen on the edge of a narrow shelf. Its silver lettering—Perry's Pest Control, (918) 555-0183, The Critter Getter of Tahlequah, Oklahoma—and the large, round size of the pen's body grabbed my attention—more so the matched silver clasp and tip and clicker; too, the body was earthy brown, near copper I'd say. I picked up both the pen and the movie behind it: *Dance Me Outside*.

At home I slid the movie into my VCR, made a pitcher

of that too-sweet tea, and fell into my recliner. Sissy walked into the house a little too chipper.

"What's Turtle watching today?" she asked, like I was one of her bubbly little friends instead of her mother. She plopped onto the couch, and I didn't bother to turn around because I was reading the names off the opening credits. The phone rang across the room, forcing Sissy to hop from the couch. She snatched the phone off the wall, pulled the cord to one side.

"Tank?" she asked. I'm not sure why she called him that. Come to find out, his name was Toby. Then she paused, and said, "No, I don't speak Spanish." She listened until the person finished speaking and then, rudely, she hung up the phone. The word *Spanish* made me think of my husband and I wanted to ask if it was him. Instead, I kept watching *Dance Me Outside*.

Ever came home forty or forty-five minutes later. The movie was not over yet, and it was starting to get good. Sissy told Ever she got a phone call about their father, my Everardo, and I couldn't believe my ears when she said he had passed away. I quickly glanced away from the movie and at my children. Ever shrugged his shoulders as he lifted his brow. The same way his father lifted his brow. He said that he had gotten a job at Greenleaf Nursery—a three-hundred-acre nursery outside of Tahlequah, across the highway from Lake Tenkiller, tucked away deep in the Ozark Hills. Sissy took this moment to announce that she was four months pregnant. The news of my daughter's pregnancy unnerved me more so than their father's death, maybe less so, but too much news made me shake. Things always happened in threes and suddenly it was like being pulled into three different directions. I was overwhelmed. So I pushed the stop button on the VCR and went into my room, where I took the Critter Getter pen out of my back pocket and placed it on the dresser.

I SPENT MOST days printing labels in the medical records department, in a back room at W. W. Hastings Indian Hospital, then pasting those labels into countless files on countless people living inside and outside of Tahlequah. Mostly Cherokees, but other tribes also, like Creeks and Seminoles, or mixed tribes, like myself, half Kiowa and half Cherokee. It's not uncommon, too, for people in this part of Oklahoma to be mixed with white and Black, and occasionally, like my children, half Mexican. Everardo had been a seasonal farm worker from Chihuahua until we married and he stayed in Oklahoma, until he changed and went back. That week I crossed my daughter's file, Yolanda Chavez, DOB: 7/15/1979, only sixteen years old and she had her first prenatal appointment. I pasted the label for the day of the appointment onto her appointment sheet and slid the file back onto the shelf with the thousands of others. I was going to be a grandmother before my fortieth birthday.

Today, I turn forty. Sitting in my car, I write today as I have on every birthday. But I don't have sheet paper. But I found a roll of paper towels in the backseat of my car.

The disappointment of Sissy pregnant at sixteen held my tongue to the roof of my mouth. So we did not talk.

Days later, it was my daughter who made the first comment. She said that the pen was ugly and reminded her of a rolled turtle spread across a country road. I hardly noticed the scratches on the pen's side and if I had been talking to her, I would have told her it was my pen so she didn't need an opinion. Maybe this was what she wanted, since there were moments in the evenings before bed when she would ask me if she should be showing more and if her stretch marks would go away. "Why did the nausea stop and the heartburn start?" she'd ask. "Will my hips get too wide? Why are my breasts so tender?"

Her body changed with the summer heat until both were unbearable. She asked if I wanted to feel the baby move or see her belly button sticking out, but I'd pour myself a glass of tea and go into my room. At times a sob slipped from under her breath and other times a sigh escaped from her gritted teeth. Either way I'd leave my daughter to sit by the phone and wait for this Tank person to not call. Because he never did. Well, maybe not never, but almost never. If you asked me, it might as well have been never.

In the evenings, I watched my shows on television. Ever would walk through the front door around five thirty. He always took a nap for an hour or so. Working under the sun cooked him into submission. It broiled him from a light-colored skin to an earthy copper to a dark brown. He had little energy until after his nap and dinner. Like Sissy, he had only ugly words about my favorite pen, said, "You're going to be one of those hoarders in your old age. Get rid of it already." Nonsense to my ears as far as I was concerned, seeing that he had no use for a pen like mine anyhow, seeing how he cared more for violence than anything else. His work at Greenleaf Nursery led him to a Cherokee man, half Creek. My son liked to call him Boo Right. At first I thought he said Bull Rights, near appropriate, but from what I understood Boo Right was some kind of playful variation of Barnett, the man's last name. I'm not sure how my son came up with that one. Anyway, Ever liked Boo Right, even though he was twenty years older. By my estimation he was the kind to drive over to Arkansas, get himself a tattoo, and come back strutting around like a chicken dancer at contest. Turned out Boo Right was an ex-con who charmed my son with comments like, "I get the urge to attack people," "sometimes you just have to fight," and "my knuckles are begging for a brawl." Ever's father had often used similar words. It seemed the older Ever grew, the more aggressive he became, and maybe he'd end up like so many other men, like Boo Right. The two would drive around the three hundred acres of Greenleaf Nursery on something called a wingding and pull orders, picking up plants, from half-gallon buckets of flowers to fifteen-gallon buckets with trees. Ever routinely tried to out-lift Boo Right with the heavier plants, so his muscles always ached. He wore a back brace, gloves, and goggles, a face mask for the areas with chemical spray. He'd come home for dinner, take a nap, and then shower before he left to go hang out with his friends. I would keep watching my shows.

Sometimes I had to turn the television up because I could not stand to hear my daughter on the telephone, chatting away with this Tank person, or more likely chatting to her friends *about* this Tank person. It was more the near begging from her, when he refused to come to the house and visit, when she believed his lies about the reasons. It made me ashamed, because her father had told me similar lies and empty promises. I almost said something when this Tank told her that he had a surprise for her birthday, but my tongue stayed against the roof of my mouth. She was excited enough to almost hug me. He would be by the house and spend the entire day with her, supposedly. The surprise, unfortunately, for her, was that her birthday came and went without any word, until later in the evening when he called to tell her that he was having car trouble. Her eyes were red from crying. Bags under those eyes. Tissue littered her room. She told him, "It's okay," holding her hand to her chest, clinching her shirt, pressing her fist, adding, "I understand." I wanted to snatch the phone and yell into the receiver, "You are worthless!" and hang up and then yell at my daughter, "Forget about him!" and hold her, saying, "You're too good and too beautiful." Instead, I turned up the television when she laughed at one of his jokes and chatted with him as if he had done nothing at all.

On my lunches at work, I would go down to the basement floor of the Indian Hospital and sit outside on a patio at the only table. I always drank exactly one can of Pepsi and thought about my son. In the mornings he made six sandwiches, three for himself, three for his friend. He packed two bottles of diet Mountain Dew so he could share his lunch and sit in his car in the broiling afternoon sun with Mr. Boo Right. When news broke about the Oklahoma City bombing, he and Boo Right were eating lunch. Initially, he thought the announcer was lying to impress the audience, mistaking the announcer's nervous pitch as fake. "Cheap guy," my son said. It was too far-fetched to believe so he said back to the radio, "You don't have to lie." Like it was the *War of the Worlds* radio show that had tricked people into believing the planet was being invaded by aliens. This time there was no trickery. Oklahoma City had been bombed.

I heard of the bombing later on the evening news after work. I never understood the rage coming from men, and likely never will, or how men abused men and then called children collateral damage. There were times when I would think of him at his lunch, while on my own, until I finished my can of Pepsi and went back upstairs to the medical records department so that I could type and paste labels for the files.

Toward the end of the summer, when Sissy was seven months along, she began to talk in detail about everything even though I didn't respond. She told me how Tank owned a brand-new truck, had his own apartment at seventeen, and would inherit his father's auto-body shop. I cared little about how Tank led Stomp Dances and had the best turkey call east of the Ozark timberline, or how he had his own stickball team. I certainly didn't want to hear about him playing basketball for the University of Oklahoma with a full scholarship. What I wanted to know was why he never introduced himself to me and why he never came around to see my daughter now that her stomach was bigger than the water tower on the Sequoyah High School grounds. Mostly, I wanted to know why my daughter let someone lie to her so often. I wanted to know so much, but my tongue was trapped behind my teeth and stuck to the roof of my mouth.

When my son spoke about Boo Right, it often had something to do with the time he spent in the Oklahoma State Penitentiary. Boo Right spent exactly eleven years, nine months, and three days incarcerated. My son learned all kinds of criminal behavior from this new friend, so I tuned my son out when he mentioned how this Mr. Boo Right knew how to cook crank. All this even though Boo Right had nearly exploded his own heart from an addiction to that stuff. I hated to hear about those awful acts. I watched my shows instead of listening to the fact that Boo Right, who must have been in his late thirties, nearly my own age, liked to fight the teenage gang members in Stilwell after spending half the night in bars with women that my son described as "that two a.m." Come to find out, Boo Right had invited him to do a little boxing in his backyard, and I wanted to say, "You need to stay home," but Ever explained that he could "take" this friend and laughed. I was less than half his size and he was more than twice as mean. It was hard for me stop his aggression. I did my best to dream of ways to keep him home, to somehow force him to stay. When that didn't work, all I had in me was to hope he'd return. So instead of saying, "It's safest at home," I watched my shows. He did return home later that night, with the left side of his face bruising from brow to chin by the following morning.

The first words I finally said to my daughter in over three months were, "Hurry up and get in the car!" She walked into the house one evening with her hands pressed to the underside of her massive belly, tears falling out of her eyes, and choking back sobs. She drove an hour-long trip with contractions, nearly driving off the road several times, crying uncontrollably against her pain—more the pain in her heart rather than the pain in her stomach.

The doctors in the emergency room at the Indian Hospital often treated people as though they were files to be read, labeled, and put back on a shelf. This doctor was rude, distracted, callous, and he stared at my daughter's file instead of her face. He gave her medication to slow the contractions and steroids for the baby inside her so that its lungs would grow faster. My daughter's body was trying to go into premature labor at seven months and her baby didn't yet have lungs. Regardless of his uncaring nature Sissy was thankful the callous doctor was able to slow her contractions.

She lay in a hospital bed, the gown tight over her high stomach, as I sat in a worn-out chair, and she said that she had gone to the Stomp Grounds that evening. She had not heard from her Tank in over two weeks. She found his friends at the Stomp that night but not him. One of his friends explained that Tank had not been coming to the Stomps for the past two months. He spent all his time with a girl, who my daughter knew well enough to call a friend, who also knew that my daughter was pregnant.

They told us my daughter could go into labor at any moment. Two weeks later she did.

This was as momentous as when my son returned home from work a few days after his nephew was born and said, "I'm joining the Army." He went on to explain that Boo Right had arrived at work that morning drunk from the night before and he nearly crashed the wingding into a greenhouse. Once almost driving off the side of a hill. His friend called him a bitch for the entire morning. His friend threatened to bruise up the other side of his face and repeatedly taunted him with the word "sqaw-nee," and told him that he wasn't a "real" Cherokee because he was a half Mexican. Boo Right went on lunch break and never came back. Ever was then responsible for pulling orders by himself for the rest of the day, which meant loading and unloading all the plants, tagging and organizing plants by docks and trucks, driving and searching hundreds of acres for special orders. By the time my son came home from work he was exhausted and had decided that he would never return to Greenleaf Nursery again. Instead, my son was joining the Army. I was relieved to say the least, and excited Ever wouldn't be following this Boo Right person into the state penitentiary.

Over the next two weeks I spoke to my daughter in small bursts, like, "It's hot outside," or "I'm hungry," or "There's nothing on TV," and she replied accordingly, which built up to longer bursts, even full sentences. By the time she went into labor I was explaining to her what she might expect while giving birth, like they would only let her eat ice chips, no matter how thirsty, and she would hurt all the way from her lower back down into her legs, even with medication. Afterward she would want to sleep for days, which she did, as I took care of my first grandchild, a grandson, who had my husband's bold eyes and my downward curving lips. In that moment, I was no longer disappointed in my daughter—instead I was proud. She did her best to find this Tank person, calling all his friends to announce the arrival of his son, calling his house every night for two weeks straight. Tank conveniently never visited and allowed his parents to deal with my daughter, who told her, "That baby is not my grandchild." They requested a paternity test because according to these people, my daughter probably didn't know who the real father was. This talk ended when she did get a paternity test and this Tank person then had child support payments due every month. Served him right, and my daughter finally had her justice.

On the day my son left for basic training, before an army recruiter picked him up to take him to Oklahoma City where he would get on a bus for Fort Leonard Wood in Missouri, he held his nephew. He said goodbye like he was going to the video store in Reasor's to pick up a movie and he would be back in thirty minutes. When we said goodbye, we knew he would be gone longer, but pretended like he would be back soon.

I write today as I have on every birthday. When I climbed into my car this afternoon and drove to Greenleaf Nursery, I thought about my son. When I kept driving down the highway and headed toward Vian, I thought about my daughter, until I turned around and drove back to Tahlequah. As I sped down Stick Ross Mountain Road too fast, against bends too tight, near hills too close, with too many trees to miss one, I thought about their father. He'd died nearly six months ago, with only a shoulder shrug for a goodbye. I had not seen him in nearly five years, give or take. I myself had finally escaped his abuse, but not before he taught our children how to take the same. Today I will return this copper pen with silver lettering to the video section in Reasor's grocery store and place it back on that narrow shelf, because I see clearly now that my husband was a pen that left his ink in these paper towels that no one will ever read.

Yolanda "Sissy" Chavez
(1999)

WHEN I SAW Lonnie Nowater walk out of Black Hawk Liquor Store with one of those McCarty boys, I thought, there goes a match made in Cherokee hell. I didn't know that Lonnie and Ever were writing letters and talking on the phone. In fact, I didn't remember seeing Lonnie until Ever brought her home. Mom always said, "Don't bring a girl around my house unless you're going to marry her," and sure enough Ever introduced us to Lonnie as his fiancée. Once I met her, I suddenly remembered driving down Muskogee Avenue and seeing her walk out of the liquor store. I knew right away she was ou-yoee, like Uktena slithering out of its hole.

At the time, Ever was on military leave for two weeks and lived in single housing at Fort Sam Houston, Texas. He couldn't take her back with him. Before I had the bravery to tell him about the McCarty boy, Mom had already invited Lonnie to live inside our house.

"Sissy," my mom told me, "give her a chance. Her family treats her terrible," and I agreed. Bottom line? He wanted to marry her, and we supported him.

Perhaps I should've taken better advantage when I drove Lonnie to work. Not that I didn't. I was more busy than disinterested. I tried the best a single mother could. Especially one who was a full-time nursing student. The day I clone myself ten times over will be the best day of my life. Let me say it like this, there was a morning I turned to Kyran in his car seat and told him, "Lonnie is your ae-logi." Or she was to become his aunt, and she was living in the room across from mine, like a sister. So she might as well be called one. Kyran was only four years old, so he asked, "Ae-logi, can you take me inside with you?" when I dropped Lonnie at Burger King, where she worked. Kyran loved the playland at Burger King. We both laughed at his little question. Unfortunately, I had to take Kyran to daycare before I drove myself to the LVN classes at Bill Willis Skill Center.

Kyran called the playland at Burger King "tunnel toys." I tended to take him on Saturday afternoons and Lonnie usually waved at us as she wiped down the pop machines or swept. I spent most of my time keeping Kyran safe as he ran around with older kids, but I did see Lonnie giggling with some guy at the registers on one particular visit. He was tall and Lonnie signaled at his beard, teasing him. I didn't hear what they were saying but by the playful look on her face, I'm sure it wasn't insulting. I didn't care. People teased each other at work. I gave her the benefit of the doubt and thought, maybe they were friends the way I had male friends. I wasn't one of those who said men and women couldn't be friends. But then I overheard gawo-nisgi at school. I had just sat at a desk when my classmate, Norma, leaned over and told me, "My cousin is messing around with someone at work. But she's engaged to a guy in the Army," exaggerating the word *Army* in a hushed tone, as if the violation was that much more severe. I had to ask so I turned around. I needed to know the girl's name. Come to find out, it was Lonnie. And the military guy Norma referred to? It was Ever. And, believe me, I let her know Ever was my brother and the last oosa-tle to piss him off had the left side of his face smashed in. Just a little warning for her cousin.

Word must have traveled quickly, because all of a sudden, Lonnie quit Burger King. Next thing, I was dropping her off at Braum's a week later. She took a night shift. After I got Kyran in his jammies and read him to sleep, I'd have just enough time to wash dishes before picking up Lonnie from work.

"Kyran is in his bed," I'd tell Mom before walking out

the door. She always watched the evening news, and Kyran wasn't the type to wake after falling asleep.

Usually, Lonnie stood waiting for me on the sidewalk near the parking lot. Most of the time I pulled in front of Braum's and she'd hop into my car. Her coworkers were either locking the front doors or climbing into their own vehicles. A couple of times, when they were short-staffed, she'd be inside wiping down ice cream machines, scraping the grill, or counting the register. On those days, I sat in my car and caught up on homework. Nursing school had as much terminology as it had mathematics, and I squeezed in reading time whenever I had the chance. And of course, Kyran liked to crawl into my lap every time he saw me with a book, so waiting in the parking lot for fifteen quiet minutes was a blessing.

The night I looked up from my books and saw Lonnie and some guy smiling at each other, I didn't think much of it—at first. There were two other workers. I could see the four of them through the large open windows—like most fast-food restaurants Braum's had a big, open drive-thru window. Lonnie was clearing out a register, while the other three were cleaning. The guy danced behind Lonnie. I saw his mouth move as he said something. Lonnie leaned forward and pressed her ass against this guy's crotch. Then she jumped away laughing. It hit me right in the chest. I couldn't believe it. Sorry skee-ni little uok-seni. I shifted my car into

Drive, but then I hesitated. Surely, I was overreacting. I shifted back to Park and waited for her to climb into my car.

I asked her, "Do you love my brother?"

It was the quietest car ride I'd ever had. She must have known I saw. Maybe I should've taken a different approach, but I was shocked by it, what sister wouldn't be? At the house, we both walked straight to our bedrooms. For me it was to check on Kyran. But for Lonnie, surely it was to escape the awkwardness. This was likely the reason she'd moved to McDonald's by the time Ever came back to Tahlequah for the marriage ceremony.

CHEROKEES IN EVERY surrounding town from Locust Grove to Stilwell over to Bunch and down to Keys knew about the Nowater family. Tahlequah had the unfortunate consequence of housing them. And in a town as small as Tahlequah, no one could do anything without gawo-nisgi. Someone always knew about it before it was done. Like Kyran's father, how everyone knew before I did that he cheated on me and threw away his son. Maybe I suspected, and I had to learn the hard way: suspicions in a small town were better than truth. Lonnie and her family knew that as well as any of our families.

When someone told me about Lonnie's father, Arnold, having random people drop in at his home, I knew they were his customers. We all knew he made meth at the trailer park by the Elks Lodge south of town. Just like everyone knew that Arnold's father, BJ Nowater, cooked the mean-est Sunday moonshine. The Nowaters were the kind to go wanted and underground for years at a time; then serve time in multiple counties after they were arrested. Arnold spent years being transferred between Cherokee, Adair, and Mayes County jails. BJ did the same, and both served time for battery or larceny or distribution or a combination of all three. It was a rarity when they were both out together.

Lonnie's mother, Janetta Nowater, was a Wolfpaw by birth. How could she raise four kids when she wasn't raised right herself? Her way of keeping them in line was popping them in the mouth, until they were big enough to pop her back. Lonnie said, "Mom had the biggest knuckles," and laughed about it. Her mother was known to work on male crews at the local plant nurseries. She could throw buckets with the strongest of men for a reason. Lonnie was the old-est and took the worst of the beatings, and likely took the worst of everything else, too. When her father wasn't in jail, he was awake for days at a time, out of his mind, and way too interested in his daughters, but Lonnie most of all.

"Daddy always said I had a good mouth," she told me once, laughing. I thought, this poor girl was raised inside a pit of snakes. She always tried to act like it hadn't been a big deal, her mother smacking her around, her daddy doing anything he wanted to her.

Then one night, her mom full-on attacked her, and Lonnie's screams were so loud the neighbors called. She was picked up by Indian Child Welfare and went to live at Oaks Mission School. She was sixteen years old at the time, and she stayed until she turned eighteen. Soon after moving back to Tahlequah, she ran into Ever while he was on military leave. It was cruise night in Tahlequah and Ever had to show off the new hydraulics on his Monte Carlo. Lonnie sat with a group of girls in the parking lot where he popped three-wheel motion. Ever told me, "She was the bravest one there, asking me for a cruise up the strip." Lonnie remembered Ever's military-issue Army athletic T-shirt—gray in color—with the letters ARMY spread across his chest. I suppose that was when Ever and Lonnie started talking and writing.

EVER WAS ABOUT to begin his yearlong tour, and he wanted to marry Lonnie before shipping out. And we were behind him all the way. When the Army asked him where he wanted to be stationed, most recruits listed places close to home, but Ever's number one choice was South Korea, second was Japan, and third was Alaska. It was almost like he wanted to move as far away from Tahlequah as he could. I always wondered why he never chose Fort Sill, on the other side of Oklahoma from Tahlequah, but close to our Kiowa side of the family in Lawton.

When he signed up to go to South Korea, he hadn't expected to be marrying anytime soon. Then Lonnie came into the picture. The Army gave him two weeks of leave before he was to report to Camp Humphreys in South Korea. He decided to marry Lonnie before the tour, and then move in together afterward. I was hopeful. So was Mom. So much so, we volunteered to help. I scheduled the wedding ceremony for them at First Indian Baptist Church of Tahlequah.

Ever had it easy when it came to finding a best man; Quinton was like a brother to him.

Lonnie made a trip to Birdtail Housing Addition to stop at her mother Janetta's apartment. Janetta made Lonnie's two sisters and her brother come into the living room.

"Okay, Lonnie tell us your big news," Janetta said.

When she told them she was getting married, they all laughed. Her next youngest sister asked, "Who'd marry someone as ugly as you?" Lonnie hurried out of the apartment.

We had family coming from Lawton the night before and family in town already. Not to mention all our local friends and their family, at least a hundred people from our side. The groom's side of the church would be packed with people shoulder to shoulder, while the other side would be so vacant tumbleweed might blow through. What would our family say when the bride had no family?

We did what we could. I asked Lonnie what kind of cake she wanted, and she said, "Just big enough to feed everyone." Out of sheer desperation I called my friend Norma, from nursing school, and she agreed to be a bridesmaid along with me. Then I asked Lonnie for the color of our dresses, and she said, "What will match with white?" It was a series of confusing answers like this that told us we'd have to organize the entire wedding. Besides, Ever was paying for it so we'd better be the ones making the decisions. The last thing we needed was for Lonnie to throw a deer carcass on the dinner table.

Mom picked the color scheme—crimson, gray, and white—and I spoke to people at First Indian Baptist Church. We ordered a three-tiered cake from the bakery at Reasor's. Mom called Aunt Lila and took down Quinton's arm length and waist size, and then I rented him a nice gray suit from Downtown Bridals. Ever decided to wear his Class A uniform. Mom said to keep the meal simple, so I ordered steak and chicken dishes from Restaurant of the Cherokees.

All through the preparations, Lonnie acted like every task was a labored request, as if she was working a long shift at a chicken factory. But when she saw Ever at the airport in Tulsa, I had never seen her eyes so wide or smile so big. He walked out of the bridge from the airplane in his Class A uniform. Multicolored badges decorated the left side of his chest. His uniform was pressed so stiff, his shoulders looked as if they were as wide as a building. Kyran's smile lit up almost as bright as Lonnie's. Lonnie ran carelessly through the airport, sliding past people as she hurried toward him. She squealed. The two of them hugged in the terminal and it became a spectating event. People turned around in their chairs. Their eyes and smiles were like a spotlight on Ever and Lonnie. I think I even heard a few people sigh when they kissed.

The car ride home became borderline pornographic and I turned to Ever in the backseat and said, "Wait until we get to Tahlequah." At the house, they quietly slipped into the bedroom. Over the days leading up to the wedding, they ate off the same plate at every meal, spooned on the living room couch, and slipped into the bathroom to take showers together. Ever told Lonnie, "You won't have to deal with your family anymore," and "Mom said you can stay here as long as you like" and "This next year will go by fast."

The night they rented a movie from Reasor's, I watched as Lonnie brought Ever popcorn and then candy and then he requested a glass of Pepsi. Lonnie jumped to her feet like a broken spring tearing through the cushion. Don't get me wrong, I was happy for them. I saw how Lonnie loved Ever. But I couldn't help myself.

"Ever!" I said. "They trained you to run two miles in ten minutes but you can't walk into the kitchen to get your own food?"

I took Kyran into my bedroom because I didn't need to have him watching Ever and Lonnie spoon together during the movie—and likely worse. I'm sure this was the reason they unexpectedly decided to spend the remaining two days before the ceremony on an impromptu prewedding honeymoon in Branson.

They managed to be out of each other's arms long

enough to complete the wedding ceremony. I'm not going to lie—it was awkward standing at the front of the church as a bridesmaid with my classmate Norma. To make matters worse, me and Norma stood next to a stranger. Lonnie had met a girl a week before—soon after she started working with Lonnie at McDonald's. I always imagined the poor thing had agreed just so she could get a free meal. But there we stood. The three of us—me and Norma with some stranger—at the front of the altar.

Every pew filled and we made it a point to tell family to sit on both sides. "Don't only fill the groom's side of the church," we whispered to them. Aunt Lila and Uncle Hank arrived late the night before and brought Quinton with them. We pulled out the hide-a-bed from the sofa. Quinton slept curled up on the love seat. Ever asked him if he wanted a pallet of blankets on the floor instead, and he said, "No, I always sleep crooked anyway," and he laughed. Uncle Hayes picked up his mother, Jolene, from Cherokee County Nursing Home. I picked up Grandma Lena. She had been sharing old family stories with me for as long as I could remember, and I hoped to dig out a little more gawo-nisgi from her on the drive to the church.

Some of the guys Ever had grown up with, like Conner and Bradley, were there, along with their families. Conner's grandmother looked real hard at the medals on Ever's chest and pointed at one with wings attached to a parachute, saying, "It must have been fun getting that one." Bradley's mom gave him a long hug and said how proud she was of him. The hug wouldn't have been so bad if she wasn't built so low to the ground.

"I think she's going to fold him in half," Quinton said.

Ever managed to work through everyone in the pews, stepping around knees to get to cousins on the Stopp side of the family. "We only live out at Park Hill," our cousin Peaches said. "How come you never visit?"

I scanned the crowd of faces in search for anyone from the Nowater family. I'd hoped her mother would change her mind and arrive at the last minute. I had every pew dotted with small bouquets of white flowers, and the white streamers ran along the arms and backsides. There had to have been around a hundred people in attendance. Our Cherokee side with the Stopps made up a large portion of the numbers, but as I scanned the crowd for Nowaters, it appeared the Stopps were the only Cherokees in attendance on that day.

Well, until the wedding song.

Lonnie Nowater was a beautiful girl. I wasn't going to deny. She'd never worn makeup, and she didn't even know how to put it on. She had a naturally even brown tone to her skin, so I didn't have to perform any miracles. I applied her lipstick and contoured her full lips. I brushed on mascara to show off her almond eyes, just a little to enhance what she already had. But when she came walking down the aisle in the white dress I had picked out, there was something about seeing her with the wedding bouquet in her hands, the veil over her face, and the white train sliding behind her, that made me pause.

She met Ever at the altar along with the pastor. To be honest, I didn't hear most of what the pastor said. I saw the two of them standing there at the altar of the church and I couldn't help but think about Lonnie walking away from Black Hawk Liquor Store with one of those McCarty boys. I remembered hearing gawo-nisgi about her cheating on Ever with a coworker and then I could see in my mind's eye her pushing her ass up against another man's crotch. When the pastor said, "Speak now or forever hold your peace," it was the only part of the wedding ceremony I heard that day.

Ever smiled like a baby possum. He couldn't stop looking at Lonnie; he hadn't stopped looking at her since the airport. In that moment, it quickly became easy for me to question myself. Maybe it was misinterpretation and gossip, maybe I was being an overprotective sister, and maybe I overreacted to Lonnie's intentions. Maybe she just needed a little guidance. Numerous maybes ran through my mind until, maybe, I convinced myself of Lonnie's innocence out of hope and disillusion.

I DIDN'T KEEP Kyran from McDonald's on account of Lonnie working there; it just wasn't good for his age anymore. He was about to turn five years old, so he was at that in-between stage, where he was too big for the little stuff and too little for the rest. The only toys for his age were a fire truck steering wheel and a tic-tac-toe game. He once tried to climb into the tunnels with the older kids and lasted maybe two minutes. He froze, and then I heard him yelling deep inside the playland. I had to climb into the tunnels. The kids looked at me like I was crooked-eyed and crazy. It took me a minute, but I squeezed my way through. I found him standing to the side of a center walkway, his back to the mesh screen. The quickest and easiest way back down was the tunnel slide. I convinced Kyran to sit in front of me and we slid to the bottom, but after that, he didn't want to go to McDonald's.

Then a few months after the wedding, when we drove by McDonald's, he yelled out, "I want a big boy toy."

We found Lonnie at the register. Kyran rushed up to the counter and he reached his little hand up to signal Lonnie to give him a high five. Lonnie laughed as she slapped his hand

"What can I get for my little man?" she asked.

Lonnie took down Kyran's Happy Meal. A middle-aged white guy walked up to the register and stood beside Lonnie. He wore a button-down shirt with a plastic badge showing his name: JON. His uniform was different from Lonnie's faded black polo shirt. Jon was clearly a manager and Lonnie's boss, seeing how he wore a freshly pressed button-down shirt. His head was bald on the top and shaved around the sides, maybe forty years old with the wrinkles around his eyes. He was in solid shape, not like a bodybuilder, but muscular with enough extra weight to broaden out his body, especially his shoulders. He had a neck like a tractor tire. Thick with veins showing.

"Is this your family?" he asked Lonnie.

Kyran yelled, "This is my ae-logi!" And Lonnie explained how ae-logi meant aunt in Cherokee.

"Meals are on us," Jon said. "Don't worry about it."

I thanked him and we hurried out.

I didn't think anything about the exchange until a few weeks later. I was getting ready to pick Lonnie up from work when I saw a car pull into the driveway. I looked out the window and the same manager, Jon, was in the driver's seat. Lonnie climbed out of the vehicle. She stood at the open passenger door and talked to him for about five minutes or so. They seemed to have a lot to say to each other. Then I remembered the free meal at McDonald's.

"Do you have rides now?" I asked Lonnie when she walked inside.

"He gave me a ride today," she said. "I don't know if he'll do it again."

Then they needed her to work a late shift, so I started picking her up around eleven at night. For someone who had to wake up at five in the morning to get herself and her son ready for the day, it was difficult. Most days I was ready for bed before Kyran. One night I drove all the way to McDonald's at eleven, but she was nowhere to be seen. I pulled into the drive-thru and asked the guy at the window.

"Boss took Lonnie home about an hour ago," he said.

Two o'clock in the morning, I heard the front door open. I'm sure she would have offered me some type of explanation, but I was too tired to ask.

Soon she told me I didn't have to pick her up from work at all. Jon gave her rides. I had a lot to juggle and partially felt grateful. Between Kyran, classes, and homework, I hardly had enough time. I thought of it as Lonnie being considerate, and honestly, I figured she was getting her life together, finally. She was finding her own way.

Ever had been in South Korea a couple months when Mom started to brag on Lonnie. Mom told me how Lonnie ran the kitchen at the McDonald's, rearranged the freezers, and stocked shelves without any help, as if she were the only person in the building. Somehow she had turned into Superwoman. I was always in bed and sleeping when I heard the front door unlock. After a few nights I asked Mom, "Why is Lonnie staying out so late?" and she said, "McDonald's is starting to run twenty-four hours." Mom was convinced of Lonnie's superhuman powers and told me about how she ran registers, cooked, and handed out orders virtually all night. I thought, sign her up for Marvel comics. She was going to be our Cherokee superhero.

Normally, I woke before anyone else in the house. I'd give myself an hour to shower and have my coffee, then I'd wake Kyran to get him ready for the day. About halfway through morning breakfast, Mom would get up and start getting ready for work. I'd head to the daycare and then to Bill Willis, and Mom would drive to Hastings. Lonnie would sleep through the doors opening and closing and the dishes rattling as I prepared breakfast. But one morning, I was caught by surprise. I walked into the bathroom and saw Lonnie looking up at me from the toilet. We both mumbled some type of apology and I quickly backed out of the bathroom.

Lonnie continued to take over the bathroom first thing in the morning. She was awake three or four days out of the week over the next few weeks. Then I was surprised for a different reason: my coffee was already brewed and waiting for me in the coffee pot. I took it as another kind gesture. Maybe she'd started drinking coffee herself. Then the next morning Lonnie made my coffee again. This kept happening.

Finally I asked her. "Why are you up so early these days? Did they change your schedule?"

"No," she said. "I'm used to staying busy and it's harder for me to sleep."

By then, I had been in nursing school for a while, and I'd taken a variety of courses geared toward patient assessment. Lonnie's new behavior brought one in particular to the edges of my mind: The Signs, Habits, and Behaviors of Methamphetamine Addicts. I had no real proof, solid proof. But I wondered.

We had learned about recognizing meth addicts in their

worst stage of addiction, with the sores on their faces, their hands constantly moving, their eyes always shifting. But we had also learned the more subtle signs, the earlier stages, like the sporadic sleeping patterns and unfinished tasks. Overconfidence was another trait, so when Mom described Lonnie as nearly superhuman, I should've started to worry.

Lonnie making my coffee in the mornings may have been a cry for help. Maybe she wanted me to notice. I was a nursing student and I was being trained to inquire, but I didn't. The stress of nursing school coupled with caring for Kyran as a single parent consumed me. Mom helped me watch him so I could study in the evenings, but I handled everything else on my own. I was worn out from long day after long day; some days it was a miracle just to keep my eyes open in class. I felt like someone should've loaded me onto a hospital gurney and hooked me to an IV. But sleep deprivation was a nursing-school requirement. At home, I was too busy to think about anything other than my books and Kyran. Lonnie was a shadow on the wall I only noticed when I reflected carefully on my day, which was almost never. In hindsight, I wished I had done more for Lonnie when I started to wonder.

THEN THE DAY finally came. I had done it. I finally had my last day at Bill Willis. I walked through the front door of the house and screamed, "Holy shit!" Mom jumped up, and Kyran flinched and started crying. I ran to him and quickly scooped him up, saying, "I'm sorry, choo-ji. Mommy's just excited." I rubbed his back and squeezed him. I'd been telling myself to enroll Kyran in tumbling classes and I'd made excuses every week. Now he could finally get the attention he needed. Maybe a tear or two slipped out of my eyes. Tla, I cried harder than Kyran. We were both big ol' babies that day. I had interviewed at Cherokee County Nursing Home and my new hire date would be the Monday after I graduated. It was only an entry-level nursing job, but I would be able to provide for Kyran. I had finally done it. I was so proud of myself.

I mentioned the idea of a party to Norma. It was more of a blurt than anything, but being so relieved made us easily excitable. To finally be finished, to have accomplished something I never thought I'd be able to do, I deserved a celebration.

Norma said, "It'll be just a few of us nursing students."

The graduation was on a Friday and Aunt Lila drove up from Lawton with Uncle Hank. Mom picked up Grandma Lena, who wanted to show off her new camera. Grandma was a shutterbug buzzing around me and all my friends. She handed Mom the camera and had her take a photo of us. I faced the camera and smiled, but grandma stared at me instead. Her arm gently over my shoulder. I told her, "Grandma, look at the camera," and she echoed back, "Tla! I'm going to look at my sweet little girl all grown up." Her eyes trained on the side of my face. It was so awkward. But Grandma Lena wanted to stare at me like a psychopath. I did everything I could to keep my eyes facing forward. We all laughed as Mom snapped the picture. It was an afternoon ceremony, and afterward Mom planned to drive back to Lawton to spend time with Aunt Lila for the week. Aunt Lila would drive her back to Tahlequah the following weekend. Not only did I get to graduate but I also had the entire house to myself. Well, along with Kyran and Lonnie.

That week, I ran into Rick at the Circle S laundromat. He was a Ballard and came from good people. We'd graduated from Sequoyah High School together. We caught up with each other while folding clothes. He finished first but stayed to help me with Kryan's laundry. It was cute watching him fold those tiny shirts—sweet how hard he tried. Long story short, I invited him to come over for the party. It wasn't a large group, maybe ten or twelve of us. We decided on taco soup, chips, and salsa, along with a few cases of Pepsi.

We played Uno and Skip-Bo and then rummy, like the nursing nerds that we were. Everyone was so relieved to have school out of the way. Between games, we threw chips at each other's faces and polished off a bowl full of M&Ms. I kept laughing at Rick's white shirt because he accidentally spilled some Pepsi onto his left nipple. His dark brown areola was clear as day through the wet spot. And it didn't help when he grabbed my hand and tried to make me touch it.

I'd like to say we were silly because of the high amounts of sugar and caffeine, but honestly it was the relief of knowing we no longer had any classes.

An hour or so after we started our card games, two of Rick's friends knocked on the door. They brought a case of beer with them. It wasn't enough to get anyone drunk, but enough to make people sillier. Someone said they wanted to do travel nursing to make their way to Alaska.

"I've always wanted to go to Peru," I said and added, "But I'll need to learn Spanish."

Someone called me out on being half Mexican and not knowing any Spanish. It was true. Mom was full-blood Kiowa/Cherokee and understood Spanish perfectly, where I only knew enough Spanish to order food at a Mexican restaurant.

"That'll change when I visit Peru," I blurted out. "They'll teach me."

Time flew and soon we were all tired. We were habituated to going to bed early to wake up early for class. It wasn't even midnight before everyone took off.

Rick's two friends said they had a few too many beers and asked to sleep in the living room. I didn't want anyone getting into a car accident. By midnight, we had everyone out of the house and we'd washed the dishes. From the ceremony to the get-together to cleaning up after everyone, I was ready to crawl under my cool sheets and instantly fall asleep.

I'd drunk way too much Pepsi during the party. It caught up to me around three in the morning. I woke to use the bathroom, but I paused in front of Lonnie's bedroom door because I heard sounds. Light came through the bottom of the door. On my way back out of the bathroom, I heard the sounds again. I stepped up to Lonnie's door and leaned my ear close. Suddenly, there was a shout, or more like a yell, and it was a male voice. Rick's two friends were supposed to be in the living room. I only found the one sleeping on the couch. I thought: ou-yoee. I marched back down the hallway and I threw open Lonnie's door.

The first thing I saw was the syringe. I couldn't believe it. Lonnie sat on her bed and this guy knelt in front of her. He held the needle, Lonnie had her arm out, and this guy had stuck the needle into the basilic vein in the bend of Lonnie's elbow. They both looked at me, but they didn't stop. He finished injecting meth into Lonnie's arm before he pulled away and came to his feet. A trickle of blood came from Lonnie's arm and she quickly wiped the blood with the tip of her finger, brought her finger to her mouth, and sucked off the blood. Her eyes were wide and so were his.

"What is this?" was all I managed to say. I said it too loud and glanced over my shoulder, afraid I had startled Kyran out of sleep.

No one said anything. Suddenly, I realized Lonnie sat in her panties on the edge of the bed, and this guy had his shirt off. I didn't need to ask them why they were both half naked. In fact, I didn't know what to say or ask or yell. It felt like hours passed, but it must have been a few seconds.

"Get out of my mother's house," I finally said. "Both of you."

I wanted to slam the bedroom door shut behind me, and if Kyran hadn't been in the house I would've. I stormed into my room and shook Rick awake.

"Get your friends out of my house."

Kyran was sound asleep. I was grateful. I sat on the edge of my bed as I listened to everyone in the house. I heard Rick wake the guy on the couch and then the front door opened and shut. Rick came back into the bedroom.

"Everyone is out of your house."

"Lonnie?"

"Yes, she's out too."

LONNIE MOVED BACK to her mother's apartment. A few weeks later I saw her walking away from Black Hawk Liquor Store. I thought she was with a new guy, but when I looked at him a little closer, I realized who it was. He had a beard now. It was the manager from McDonald's. I remembered images from nursing school where beards were grown to hide meth sores. The difference wasn't only in his beard but in his body. Now? He was like a scarecrow stuck on a pole. It was amazing to see how much he had changed in such a short amount of time. His shoulders were so narrow it looked like they were bowed forward. His neck was more the size of a garden tool than a tractor tire. He was fidgety and walked with his back straight—almost like he was at full military attention.

Lonnie looked agitated, too, and had lost a lot of weight. Her beautiful almond eyes were sunken and appeared almost fishlike. Her flawless skin was now splotchy and seemed to almost sag on her face. I didn't see any sores, but she looked like she aged thirty years. Her pants were baggy and hung below her waist. She walked board straight like the guy she was with, and I could see her talking rapidly. They walked up Muskogee Avenue toward downtown, and her constant chatter didn't stop when he spoke. They simply talked over each other.

I placed my hand over my mouth and held back the tears. My heart was broken, seeing her so frail and erratic, so different.

BY THE TIME Ever folded his arms across his chest, I knew he'd listen, but I wasn't sure if he'd hear. He was uha-hnalun before I told him half of what Lonnie had done. He told me, "If someone stood at the top of the Sequoyah High School water tower, you'd be the one to push them off."

Mom stopped him. "Ever, give Sissy time to finish."

What he needed to hear about Lonnie had to come from us both. Honestly, I was a little scared of Ever. The more I told him about Lonnie, the straighter he sat and the tighter his fists clinched. He was prone to the rage he inherited from our father. At one point, he stormed into the kitchen to get a glass of water and slammed a fist on the counter. I never saw him aggressive toward women, but I had witnessed the damage he liked to do to other men. His sudden silence was the scariest moment, like when a tornado sucks out all the air just before it hits. Having my mother there gave me a certain level of reassurance.

My only regret? We should have said something sooner. Tla, we should have said something before he married Lonnie. I guess I was too hopeful. We both were. Maybe a part of us wanted to rescue Lonnie. Or hoped the best for her. There was only one thing worse than wasted potential: the people who didn't give potential any expectations. Ever learned this lesson all too well. He stormed out of our mother's house and found Lonnie Nowater. Then he lived with her long enough to discover the truth for himself.

Hank Quoetone
(2003)

CLAYTON HANDED EVER the microphone and he announced, "Can the parents of these children claim responsibility? We have five children who are in need of supervision."

Ever made the kids stand at the front of the arena. All of them lined up, looking out at the powwow, with hundreds of eyes staring back, and none of the parents claimed those kids. Gaa, must be ashamed of their kids, we thought. But it turned out the kids had walked over from Red Elk. My nephew had each of those kids give him their parents' phone numbers. He stood outside Watchetaker Hall as rattling minivans and muddy trucks pulled up to the sheet metal building. Might know, their heads dropped as soon as they seen their parents.

"Don't run around these statues," Ever had told them. "It's a memorial. Have respect for your veterans." He gets that way about military things—salutes when he walks by the U.S. flag—one of those guys. Ask him how In'dins can serve a country that's robbed us of our dignity, honor, and cultural way of life, and he'll tell you, "If you think the U.S. has that much power then you haven't been to one of our family gourd dances" and "We've been fighting to protect this land since Saynday pulled us out of a tree stump, so why stop now?"

Imagine his reaction when he walked up to the Comanche Code Talker Memorial and found one of the cement benches lying on the ground. Someone had knocked the top portion off its legs. Worse still, though—to Ever—a large edge of the bench had cracked off. An old warrior culture, Kiowa, like Comanche, were particular about how we honored our fallen soldiers. Ever was determined to find out who broke that bench. He told me, "I should've been there to stop it," as if he was stuck between shame and regret. Maybe somehow, if he found the perpetrator, he could get unstuck.

Mostly, the kids liked to hang on to the back of the WWII soldier kneeling down on one knee. They'd pretend to talk on the handheld radio in the soldier's grip.

"You'll have to keep a close eye," I told him.

"Don't worry, Say'gee."

Earlier that day, he caught two of those same kids climbing the "Spirit Talker" behind the WWII soldier and trying to touch the point of its spear. At the powwows, kids liked to play tag around the eight obelisks that surround the statue and list the names of Comanche soldiers. The kids jumped off the benches grouped in a half circle toward the back of the memorial. Ever had chased them away a good six times, but they kept sneaking back when he had to patrol the powwow. He pulled all those kids together and started to lecture, maybe even yelled a little too much because one of the younger boys sobbed and cried out, "Didn't do it!"

My son, Quinton, had been called by the Kiowa Tribe to do disaster relief down in Alabama fighting a large forest fire. Quinton and Ever were like each other's shadows, and they usually ran security together every year. This was the Oklahoma Gourd Dance Club's thirteenth annual powwow. I told my nephew to find someone to help out, but Ever had to get back on his feet. He'd get paid double if he didn't replace Quinton and he needed the money. He had been out of work for nearly three months already. He lived in our garage with his two sons and daughter. He needed a home—a place he could settle his kids. His kids needed their own bedrooms, instead of being piled on the same bed. And kids cost money, with shoes and clothes. He was a single parent. The mother to his kids was addicted to meth and could barely take care of herself, worthless. I had him roofing a little through the Comanche Nation Housing Authority, but it wasn't enough. I told him to use the money from doing security to buy some interview clothes. He needed a second person because there would be too many people. I was giving him three hundred dollars for doing security over the weekend. If he brought in someone else, he would have to split that money two ways. "It's not Red Earth," he told me, "this is a traditional powwow." A one-man job, he thought.

Then Ever bounced from one end of the building to the other like drumsticks on hide, trying to keep rhythm with the crowd. Like those two young guys—teenagers—who walked up to the powwow from I-44. Fourteen or fifteen years old, both of them. The Black kid wore a heavy shirt and baggy jeans that fell off his waist, while the Mexican kid had on a long-sleeved shirt and heavy boots that dragged the ground with each step (not the kind of clothes you wear in 100-degree weather). They came in from behind the building, and Ever stopped them.

"What are you doing back here?"

"We walked up from Lawton," one of them said.

"That's not very smart, guy," Ever said.

Turned out, they got into an argument with their girl-friends. They'd been at a party the night before and their girlfriends were flirting with other boys. There was a big fight and it ended with them walking away from the house.

Worse still, they had driven down from OKC in their girl-friends' car.

"We should've never gone to that party," the other one said.

They'd barely made it past Fort Sill. At the Love's convenience store at the Medicine Park exit, the clerk suggested that someone at the powwow might give them a ride back to OKC. Little did these young guys understand what a powwow was, how it was a place to be rescued, healed, given a second chance. Ever let them use his cell phone to call their mothers. He got them some bottled water and nachos from the concession. It was a hundred-degree weather at the beginning of June and they looked dehydrated and burnt out. It was so hot that summer you wanted to stand in an ice chest, kicking around cans of Pepsi and bottles of water. They chugged down three waters each—poor things.

After Ever fed those young guys, he stayed and hung out at the concession stand, where he busted face on some nachos, too, and Monte told him about a mountain shaped like the head of an In'din chief—down to the bump in its nose. That's when a kid ran up to him. He was one of those long-haired boys around powwows you see often, likes to wear basketball gear. The kid told him about the bench. Monte told Ever to have the MC make an announcement. My nephew was more concerned with telling *me*.

"Uncle," he said. I sat next to the powwow MC at the

long table toward the front. I had to lean in close to hear him because my hearing wasn't what it used to be. Then there were the drumbeats filling the metal building. He had to yell and repeat what he said a few times.

I yelled back, "You better find out who did it."

Watchetaker Hall was filled with at least three hundred people, so many different Kiowa and Comanche societies: the Kiowa Tia Piah, the Comanche Little Ponies, the Kiowa Gourd Clan, the Comanche War Scouts. There was even one from Texas. Then all those dancers, and all the family there to support the dancers and the Societies. He had to weed through everyone.

That long-haired boy stood next to Ethan's fry bread truck out in the parking lot. Might know, he was Ethan's oldest son, Virgil, the one from his first wife. Ethan told Ever that Virgil found the bench already broke when he went over to the statue to eat his fry bread.

Ever had no reason to doubt Ethan. He was a good one. He'd been a cook since he could reach the top of a stove. He was a big guy with hands thicker than the fry bread he cooked; one of those guys with no neck, just shoulder muscles. He'd been a part-time bouncer at the nightclubs around Lawton, but his boss had accused him of stealing and got him fired. Good thing, though, he put a deep fryer in an old ice cream truck, and now he sold at all the pow-wows around Oklahoma—Indian Tacos the size of your head and meat pies stuffed with buffalo. One of his Indian

Tacos would have me full for two days. I'd told him once, "Go over to the Comanche Nation and get a job cooking for the elders." He said, "No, this is like a second chance for me." I understood about second chances. We all needed them. Sometimes food, like a meat pie from Ethan's food truck, was a second chance in itself.

Ethan told Ever to go and ask his cousin Gilbert. Gilbert and his wife had been sitting on the bench earlier in the day, with their newborn son in a stroller.

Ever had to wait for the drum circle to finish their set. Gilbert was the newest member. The drum leader was his AA sponsor and got him drumming as a part of his recovery. Well, since he got out of prison a year ago, anyway. He was at Big Mac in McAlester, Oklahoma, for five years. He'd gotten hopped up on meth and he went crazy. Some said he was witched. He was drinking and partying at a forty-nine and he beat his nephew so bad the right side of his head collapsed. They had to rush that poor boy to OU Medical in OKC and it was touch-and-go for a few days. Good thing the young man pulled through. Otherwise Gilbert would have been in prison for life. He'd told me, "I wish I never did any of those things," and he'd joined AA, sang with a powwow drum group, and now he had a new son. I'd told him that when his boy started walking, I'd give him one of my gourds and we could have him as Head Man at the next annual. Gilbert told Ever the bench was fine and intact when he and his wife had sat over there. They had actually sat on the same bench that broke. Gilbert said he'd seen those two young guys from OKC sitting on it.

Ever found those young guys leaning against the wall outside the building, flashing their baby faces as people passed by. "Do you know who might give us a ride to the City?" the Black kid asked as soon as Ever walked up. Ever didn't know anyone going that direction. He asked them about the bench. They sat on the bench for a little while to rest their feet, they said. Walking up I-44 nearly killed them. The bench had been fine when they were there.

Ever pointed across the parking lot and down the road at a building off in the distance. "That's the Comanche police department. It's attached to the fire department. They should be able to help you get back to the City." He could tell those boys hadn't broken the bench. They just wanted to get home.

Ever ran into Clayton at the urinals. Clayton had MCed our annual powwow for nearly six years. We'd thought last year was going to be his final one because of what happened. We always had the powwow at the outdoor arena, if the heat allowed us. The year before we thought it was a good year to be outside. But a heat wave came like a tornado in the night and rushed over southern Oklahoma. We soaked bandanas in ice water and patted ourselves down. We ate ice chips left and right. But Clayton: he's a smoker, a coffee drinker, and can't resist Ethan's cooking any better than any of us. I'd been sitting next to him when he reached over and grabbed my arm. He dropped the microphone onto the table. Then he fell out of his chair. My wife nearly had a heart attack herself, watching her cousin collapse like that. I came down to his side, holding him while he clutched his chest, taking short breaths. After the ambulance came, we ended the powwow early. This year we'd moved the powwow inside Watchetaker Hall. Clayton had stopped smoking and he now turned down Ethan's cooking. He still drank coffee, but who could blame him for that one. As they walked out of the restroom, Clayton suggested hanging out near the Code Talker Memorial to see if the perpetrator came back to try and fix the bench.

Ever went back to the Memorial. He lifted the bench back off its legs and laid it in the grass so that the perpetrator would believe the bench hadn't been discovered. He walked across from Watchetaker Hall to the Comanche Complex and stood outside of the doors, leaning against a wall, and waited. He was out of sight and in the shadows. Suddenly, someone came around to check out the bench. It was me. I was there to assess the damage. Ever walked over and explained what he was doing. I thought it a good idea, but I needed him to do something for the family.

"Can you check the parking lot for Daniel's truck?" I asked him. I'd seen his son, Pauleppy, getting ready for the fancy dance competition. My daughter had been dating Daniel off and on for nearly three years already. He hit her and threatened her—jealous—always asking who she was with and what she was doing. He'd left her a few months back, and she'd gone into a bad depression, took a bottle of pills and ended up in a psych ward for a few weeks. But she'd finally wised up and told Daniel she was giving herself a second chance. She kicked him out of her life. I didn't want him around causing trouble and bringing worry to the family at our annual powwow.

Ever walked the parking lot. He called me on his walkie-talkie. "I went down every aisle," he said, "it's a negative on a red truck." Then he went back to his hiding spot over at the Complex and waited in the shadows for his perpetrator to return.

He watched the sun slide over the western edge of the Southern Plains so the night engulfed him, Watchetaker Hall, and the Comanche Complex. Under the cover of darkness, Ever caught the outline of Ethan's son—more the long ponytail running down his back—and the gleam of the Nike symbol from his basketball shorts. Behind the blinking lights of fireflies, Virgil ran up to the bench and tried to pick it up. It was too heavy for him. He tipped it onto its side and pushed it next to the cement legs. He was trying to slide one side of the bench onto the legs when Ever flipped on his flashlight and aimed it at his face.

"What are you doing?"

Virgil dropped the bench and stared at Ever like he was Deer Woman. He didn't say anything.

Ever asked him, "Does your dad know you did this?"

The boy started crying right away and shook his head: no. He fell to his knees and started begging Ever not to tell Ethan. Tears fell down his face.

"Please, Ever," he cried, "I should've never jumped between those benches."

You have to understand something about Virgil; he lives out of state with his mother. He only sees his father in the summers. His mother married a Seminole man from Florida, so they lived on the Big Cypress Reservation. Ethan didn't have the money to go out there very often. Virgil was down on his knees, looking up at my nephew.

Ever said, "Get up on your feet. Don't ever let people see you like that."

He told the boy to go back inside Watchetaker Hall or else Deer Woman was going to come out of the night and carry him away.

"Don't worry. I'm not going to say anything," he told the boy. Virgil wiped his eyes, thanked my nephew, and hustled toward the building.

Ever leaned down and heaved the broken bench back onto its cement legs.

Sometimes I wonder why my nephew gets all gung ho about military things. Some people said he left the military because he couldn't handle taking orders, and then some said he was talking back to his superiors and they more or less fired him. He always had a problem with aggression. The family worked together to settle his anger. So yeah, he was a little hotheaded sometimes. But I knew that wasn't the reason. He told me, "I couldn't believe I was with those AWOLs." There must have been close to twenty or more of them. "It was getting worse, Say'gee," he said, "I should've never done what I did to Lonnie. I was shamed."

They'd had him at Fort Sill for about three days, waiting to go before an NCO. He told me they stood in a line, down a long hallway, and each soldier walked into a room to tell why they went AWOL. When he stepped inside the office there was barely enough room for him to stand, because of a large desk taking up most of the space. He told them he was having marital issues, that the mother to his kids had a real bad addiction to meth. They asked him if he wanted to stay enlisted, and he told them, "No, because the issues haven't been resolved." And just like that he was given a regular discharge and sent on his way.

Ever held that chunk of cement in his hands, turned it around a few times, and then sat down on the bench near the Code Talker Memorial. He faced the back of the Spirit Talker portion of the statue, which hovered over the WWII soldier kneeling down on one knee with the handle of a CB radio in its grip. Ever sat there for a good while staring at the memorial.

Later that week, I had to grab a tool from a drawer in my garage. Even though we'd converted it into a bedroom for Ever and his three kids, I kept one shelf and drawer for my tools. I saw Ever place that chunk of cement on his dresser, so I asked him about it. That's when he told me about his ex-wife, Lonnie.

"It was my fault," Ever said, "I tormented Lonnie every day with every name. I called her a whore, slut, and anything I could think of. Then she ran back to meth, she ran back to the men who supplied it to her." He held up the chunk of cement. He said, "I thought I was bad before, but after the military I was worse. I actually thought it would be better than landing in prison. But it turned out to be a different piece to the same puzzle."

He insisted on paying for the bench out of his own pocket. I tried to pay myself, but he wouldn't hear it. Turned out to be exactly three hundred dollars.

Araceli Chavez
(2005)

MY TIO, EVERARDO, used to say to me, "Araceli, why you don't speak Oklahoma?" and then he'd say, "The road is wine-dy-er than a snake's belly," with the biggest smile. He loved Oklahoma as much as the Oklahomans. I liked telling stories about my uncle porque he embraced Oklahoma like no one else. Just listening to him speak was a carnival ride. He dropped an Okie "suppose so" with a Mexican "wey," saying "Suppose so, wey," and kept speaking Spanish without a pause. But there was one thing I didn't like when telling stories about my tio: I eventually had to mention his pinche baboso son, Ever Geimausaddle.

I stopped claiming Ever as a cousin when he didn't show up to his father's funeral. What kind of son does that to his father? Years after, he tried to tell me, "Araceli, you don't understand everything." But I stopped him right there porque I already knew he was not a good son. I didn't want to hear his excuses. Besides, Ever was one of those cabrones who had kids here and there. His second wife, Jimena, pobrecita, was like a little sister to me. And their daughter came into this world to carry us all on her back. Jimena said her daughter's tiny hands built a house large enough for us all. I wanted to hold Jimena, or hold onto the little girl she once was, who I knew best, but she slipped from my arms before I had grip.

Jimena's family, the Mendozas, emigrated from Chihuahua to Oklahoma the same year as my father and my uncle Everardo. My parents were farmers and her parents owned one of the first Mexican restaurants in Lawton, La Cocina. They bought their vegetables and fruits from us. Jimena was six years younger than me. When I was sixteen years old and carried crates of tomatoes through the backdoor of La Cocina, Jimena would throw her dolls to the floor to carry crates with me. I held one side while she held the other. I wanted to remember her as the little girl who helped me pull crates off the back of my apa's truck. Then ten years later she told me about meeting some Mexican-Indian guy. Then she introduced me to my own cousin. I tried to tell her about Ever, but people acted stupid when they were in love. The size of her heart grew big enough to close her ears.

She'd invited me and my family to eat dinner with her at La Cocina. It was off Eleventh Street—between Mattie Beal Park and Lee Boulevard. I pulled our SUV into the parking lot, and there Jimena stood all pressed up against Ever. As soon as I saw Ever lean in for a kiss, I hit the horn as hard as I could. They flinched. I smiled and laughed. The horn was loud enough to draw attention from people at the Whataburger across Eleventh street. I rolled down my window.

"Ever, where are your kids?"

"Araceli!" Jimena yelled at me. "Basta!"

Inside La Cocina, my mocking smile did nothing to diminish her glow. She almost floated through the restaurant and it seemed as if she glided down into the chair. Don't get me wrong, I wanted her to be happy. But I knew what Ever had to bring. My kids and husband chuckled at me as I tried to get Jimena to hear me say "He has three kids already" and "You should see how he treats his family." She paused long enough for me to run out of air.

"He's taking me to Mexico," she told me.

Ever finally had a good job working with at-risk Indio kids in Lawton. I didn't remember where it was located or the name, but it was a group home. He'd already taken Jimena on several trips to Oklahoma City. She had met his mother and sister in Tahlequah. But this trip to Mexico was the first one I heard about beforehand. The others were after she returned.

"I convinced him to visit his abuelos," she said. "Your abuelos."

"I don't think my grandparents need to be in the middle of family drama," I said.

Later that night, after I put the girls to bed, I called my father.

"You remember your uncle Everardo as someone who brought you mazapan from Mexico," my father said. "My brother was different to you than he was to me. And different still to his own children."

I let out a breath like I was punched in the stomach porque we both knew Ever didn't go to his own father's funeral.

"I'm the one who set up the visit," he said.

"Why would you do that? My abuelos are too old."

"Jimena asked me. She's a good girl. Jita, listen to me: Some things are bigger than you."

But I held on to old family resentment like a piece of earth holds on to a tombstone. When Jimena's daughter was born, my father's words became a slicing echo in my heart.

JIMENA TOLD ME how driving into Mexico felt different with Ever because it was like bringing a part of my tio back to his parents. They didn't run into any issues with federales at the Mexican border or anywhere along the drive through Chihuahua. They got a "Where are you going?" and "How long are you going to stay?" and that was it. A few hours down Chihuahua's Highway 16, they drove into Aldama.

Seeing the restaurants and convenience stores, Ever assumed it would be all dirt roads and desert mountains. Jimena laughed and said, "You watch too many movies."

The sun had set an hour before they pulled into my grandparents' driveway. It wasn't until the next day when Jimena could see the large mountains nearby. My abuelos lived in Villa Aldama and it was a little more central and an older part of the town. Their home was a pink adobe atop cement walls, and it reminded Jimena of her own grandparents' home in Placer de Guadalupe, about an hour away. There were no hallways. Each room sat directly next to each other with a doorway between. You walked into the dining room slash kitchen. The next room to the south was a living room. Then a bedroom sat to the west of the living room followed by a bedroom back to the north. So the second bedroom was really to the west of the kitchen, but there was no door connecting. The home's bathroom was the next to the last room in the house and to the west of the second bedroom. It all flowed in one direction. Later, Jimena and Ever realized they'd have to walk through my grandparents' bedroom to use the restroom.

The next morning my grandmother told Ever he had his father's eyes and when Ever smiled politely she said that Ever also had his smile, which always showed too much of his upper gumline. She stopped herself from crying by putting something to cook on the stove and told them how Everardo was teased a lot when he was kid for having that smile.

"But your father liked to be teased," she added. "He smiled as big as he could just so people would tease him. Your father was my clown and loved to make the family laugh."

It was my grandfather who asked Ever why he didn't go to his father's funeral, and my abuela tried to make him shut up. She even threatened to kick him out of the house if he didn't stop harassing their grandson. "This might be our only chance to see him," she said.

"I couldn't do it," Ever said and then walked outside.

My abuelo didn't push it anymore.

My grandmother thought that Jimena looked a little pale so she added a little extra breakfast on her plate. Jimena laughed it off as an old lady overreacting, but ate every bite.

She knew all the signs because I had told her about everything when I had my kids. She was just a goofy little teenager back then, but I'd thought she needed to know. It wasn't that I didn't want her to have children, but not too young. There were too many kids having kids. But now she was twenty years old and she was getting questioned by my grandmother for looking sick. Then the next day my abuelos sent them to buy some bottles of Coca-Cola for dinner. Jimena called Ever an "old man" because he was six years older and challenged him to a foot race.

"I bet your knees give out before we get to the store," she told him.

"Okay, on the count of three. Three!" And he took off running.

Jimena darted after him. She gained ground on him quickly and was about to race past him when she suddenly felt too tired. She slowed and then stopped altogether. She had to rest with her hands on her knees to catch her breath.

She shook it off and didn't think much about losing the race, not until later in the evening when they sat down with my grandparents and my abuela's brother. They ate slices of pork slow-cooked in a pit marinated with achiote seasoning, and fresh pork rinds in a brown paper sack. Ever teased Jimena, "I know it's good, but where are you putting all that food?" By then, she'd eaten three plates of food.

"I don't know why I'm so hungry," she said just before asking if she could have some of the pork rinds.

My abuela said, "Yes, eat all you want," and squeezed Jimena's cheeks. She kissed her on the forehead.

"This might be my only chance to feed my great grandchild."

Jimena looked curiously at her and then she translated for Ever. My grandmother laughed with delight and scooped more pork onto Jimena's plate.

The next morning, Jimena and Ever could hardly break away for the drive back to Oklahoma. My abuela kept trading hugs with them.

"You better bring my great grandkids with you next time," she told Ever.

Then she turned to Jimena. "Take care of yourself so my newest baby has better brains than her father and grandfather," she said and rubbed Jimena's stomach.

She turned back to Ever and hugged him. "You tell your kids they have a great-grandmother in Mexico waiting for them."

She turned back to Jimena. "Araceli will be a good aunty, so let her have plenty of time with your first child." Okay, I made the last one up, but that's how my grandmother always acted. She was good about holding on to people and saying goodbye for as long as she could. My grandfather eventually started rubbing her shoulders and begged her to let Jimena and Ever start back on the road to Oklahoma.

Jimena and Ever did not say a single word about my abuela's comments until they were in customs check on the United States border. The U.S. Border Patrol had them park and get out of their vehicle. They were in a tiny waiting room sitting on plastic chairs for hours.

"Do you think you might be pregnant?" Ever asked her.

Jimena had assumed my grandmother just wanted more great grandchildren, but Jimena had slept more than usual, as well. She had had an excuse for that one, too, blaming my grandparents' bed.

Now Jimena and Ever stood at a window in the waiting room of the customs office and watched as officers ran mirrors underneath Ever's car. They rummaged through the trunk. Then they pulled their luggage out and laid the bags on the sidewalk, and the officers dug around in their clothes.

They were pulled into a small room where an officer actually asked them if they were American citizens. He wore a combat uniform with a sewn badge on the left breast. This guy only wanted to harass them because Jimena said he didn't wait for them to answer. He turned to Ever. "So you were in the Army?"

"I did a year tour in Korea."

"I didn't know we were at war with Korea."

"We have a base there."

"Why aren't you in Afghanistan?"

"I discharged two years before 9/11 happened."

"Yeah, we pulled up your DD 214."

"Then why are you asking me all these questions?" Ever asked. "You probably already know my grandfather was a decorated war veteran who served in the Korean War, and you probably already know I'm Native American."

"Probably," he said and then walked out of the room without saying another word. He walked back into the room about ten minutes later and asked, "So your name is Everardo Carrillo Chavez?"

"Not anymore."

"I noticed," the officer said. "Why did you change it? Who are you hiding from?"

"I'm not hiding from anyone. I changed my last name

to my mother's maiden name, to my grandfather's name, to the last name of the family who stuck around long enough to raise me."

The officer laughed and turned back around to leave the room. The slamming door was the only thing to cut off the sound of his laughter.

Jimena took his hand and ran it over her stomach. She told him, "We'll get a pregnancy test once we make it back to Lawton."

I started to have more sympathy for Ever after learning what the border patrol did to him. And I was coming to understand that my uncle Everardo didn't really raise his kids. Maybe he was an asshole, but still, if Ever was a decent human being he should've shown up to his father's funeral. Ever hadn't needed to show up for his father, but for his father's family. He should have showed respect to his family—his cousins, his aunties, his uncles, and most of all his abuelos—who had just lost their son.

As soon as they drove back into Lawton, Jimena went straight to Wal-Mart. She went through six pregnancy tests. She didn't believe it, or couldn't believe it. I'm sure it was the thought of facing her parents. She kept wondering about a false positive so she paid another $50 to hear a doctor tell her she was pregnant. She took the printed results from Comanche County Memorial Hospital to her father and handed it to him. He reacted in a way she never expected: He shook his head and laughed and told her, "Your mother will be very happy." And when her mother said, "It took you long enough, jita," Jimena was confused. She was only twenty years old. Her parents had hoped she would marry the same age they had, which was sixteen. By the time she turned twenty, they had more or less given up on having grandchildren. Then it was Jimena's turn to laugh.

At the Indian Hospital after the four-month sonogram, they learned their baby would be a girl and then the nurse said that there looked to be a little extra fluid in the womb, and then she sighed and added, "But it's a good pregnancy." Jimena later recounted those words to me several times over. And so when Jimena was eight months, she and Ever walked into the ultrasound studio expecting to hear everything was good. But the ultrasound tech had a look of worry and told Jimena and Ever to talk to their doctor right away, who told them that the baby had a form of dwarfism. It was a shock, but it wasn't anything they couldn't handle. But their doctor turned the situation into something terrible quick. "I want you to go see a specialist today," he said.

Jimena and Ever looked at each other confused. Why the urgency? They drove to OU Medical Center in Oklahoma City. Jimena called me on the drive to help calm her nerves. She was so agitated, her thoughts spun like the revolving doors at the hospital entrance.

I remember how Jimena described the specialists at the hospital because their names were almost the same, Dr.

Singer and Dr. Singh. Dr. Singer was a tall white lady who had a soft smile to go with her soft brown hair. Dr. Singh had a stiffness to her shoulders and was from Northern India and spoke better English than most Oklahomans.

"Is my baby okay?" Jimena asked, as everybody sat at the table with her.

The doctors looked at each other. Then Dr. Singh explained that her baby had a form of dwarfism called thanatophoric dysplasia, meaning that her body was proportionately smaller than other forms of dwarfism. Her whole skeletal structure and her organs would be smaller. But since her lungs were the last organ to develop and her ribcage was so small, the lungs didn't, or couldn't, develop fully.

"What does that mean?" Jimena asked.

"Your baby's lungs will be too small," Dr. Singer said.

Dr. Singh added, "She won't survive after she's born. She won't be able to breathe once outside the womb. I wish there was more we could do, but even with all the advances we've made in recent years, this is one of those rare circumstances where we can't help."

Jimena told me about the silence from the doctors afterward. It felt like a noiseless vacuum, like her ears stopped working. My pobrecita was in shock. Who wouldn't be? And those doctors didn't do her right. A mother just learned her baby wasn't going to survive. And then they do nothing?

After days and days of crying, Jimena couldn't cry anymore. Finally, she asked Ever, "What about your medicine people?"

Ever's great-grandfather, Jasper Geimausaddle, had been a well-known medicine man in Kiowa and Comanche circles. Even though he passed away over fifty years ago, people in the community still remembered him. No one in Ever's family could sneeze without mentioning their relation to him. Kiowas held on to lineage like legacy was redemption. Porque Kiowas knew their ancestors by name, y porque Kiowas remembered their ancestors through song and dance, and most of all service, like a curandero healing for honor.

Ever's aunt Lila contacted a Kiowa medicine man from Gotebo to hold a ceremony at her house. As soon as they parked next to the curb outside, all the worry drained to Jimena's feet, into the road, and spilled down into the flood grates on the Lawton streets. Inside, they all sat in the living room: Jimena, Ever, and Ever's family; Lila, Hank, and their son, Quinton. Ever's family had brought tobacco, a Pendleton blanket, and cash for the medicine man. It was just after dinner, so the smell of goulash and fry bread filled the house.

The medicine man was much younger than she had expected. She thought he would have long gray hair and walk with a cane. Ever told her, "You watch too many movies," and laughed. Instead he had short hair and it was dark black. He couldn't have been more than forty. If so, he looked very young for his age. He dressed in regular street clothes with jeans and a solid color shirt, as if he had just clocked out at work and drove straight over to see Jimena, which may have been the case.

He placed two chairs from the dining table facing each other and invited Jimena to sit with him. Everyone else stayed in the living room. No one dared turn around to look. They stared at the television and pretended like there wasn't a ceremony happening behind them.

Jimena didn't understand the prayers and they were so quiet under his breath she could barely hear the Kiowa words. He had her drink tea from a jar, very bitter, and it was a half-quart-sized jar.

"Do I drink all of it?" she asked. He nodded and smiled.

Ever, Lila, Hank, and Quinton never took their eyes off the television.

Then the medicine man jabbed a hand behind her shoulder blade, and it felt like his fingers slid through her skin inside her upper back. His fingers wrapped around something, he yanked, and a stringy substance started streaming out of her body. He strained with each tug, and with each pull the string grew longer. He had a bucket next to her chair and he dropped the string inside. It was cottony, long, and yellow in color. She had never seen anything like it before. After nearly fifteen minutes of pulling this string, he stopped and moved to her lower back. This time he stabbed his fist, but it felt like a straw, round, thick, and hollow, against her skin. He put his mouth to his hand and started to suck. He sucked out a clump of black and brown feathers and then coughed the feathers into the bucket. He paused, caught his breath, and then sucked again. He did this over and over. Each time he paused to cough out feathers.

Ever and his family never turned around, never dared look.

As she left, he gave her a glass jar filled with the same dark tea and told her to drink it over the next four days. On the drive home, Ever didn't ask what the medicine man had done, but Jimena couldn't contain herself. She described every detail.

The medicine man met Jimena back at Ever's aunt's house every day for the next four days, where he said hushed prayers under his breath with a hand on her shoulder. She drank the tea as he instructed. She was willing to do anything and everything for her baby.

If my family had anything to say about Jimena visiting a medicine man, they never dared say anything to me. The doctors had told her her baby was going to die. What would any mother do? This medicine man was a good curandero, and I wouldn't have put up with anyone trying to spit out the word *brujo*. My family, and the Mendozas, kept whatever thoughts they may have had to themselves. And that was best for everyone—especially them—and they knew it.

After the four days, she visited Blessed Sacrament

Catholic Church over by Elmer Thomas Park. Jimena's parents were regulars at the church, like my parents, but Jimena was young and would attend a few times a year when her mother guilted her into it. I remember being like that, too. I often forgot about prayer—until I needed it.

Jimena's parents requested a private meeting with two priests, Father Ganter and Father Reed, who knew the family well, and after learning of Jimena's circumstances offered to give her a blessing. The priests escorted Jimena, her parents, and Ever from the office to the altar of the church. They placed a chair for Jimena near the pulpit, in front of the altar. Father Reed used Holy Water to bless Jimena's parents and Ever, while Father Ganter did the same and blessed Jimena. Her parents stood in front of the altar and watched Jimena with concern, their hands folded at their waists. Ever had the same look of worry. It seemed like the look washed over his face the day they heard the news and had never faded.

Father Ganter and Father Reed stood on opposite sides of Jimena, Father Ganter to her left and Father Reed to her right. They faced the altar and statue of Jesus Christ. Each placed a hand on one of Jimena's shoulders. Jimena closed her eyes.

"Gracious and loving God," Father Ganter started, and Father Reed finished, "Who has made heaven and earth." They completed the entire prayer in this echo, back and forth fashion, as Father Ganter continued, "Give health to your servant," and Father Reed echoed, "Her hope, my God, is in you." "Be to her, Lord, a tower of strength," said Father Ganter, and Father Reed followed with "in the face of the enemy."

An energy moved from her head down to her feet. By the time Father Ganter said, "Let the hand of your mercy assist Jimena's delivery, and bring her child to the light of day without harm," she felt so light it was as if she was made of air.

Jimena's parents and Ever silently stood as the priests performed the ceremony.

Jimena felt a smile grow across her lips as Father Ganter came to his final words, "May the blessing of Almighty God, the Father, the Son, and the Holy Spirit, descend upon you and your child, and remain always." Both priests finished in unison, "Amen."

Jimena opened her eyes.

The priests smiled at her smile, and she looked down at her parents and Ever. All three instantly smiled at the sight of her. The look of worry left them all.

Father Ganter gave her a bottle of holy water in a clear plastic bottle. With a hand on her shoulder, he told her to take small sips of the water every day until she gave birth. It was Father Reed who told her to not finish it all, to always leave some. She had to pray every day, too, and the priests expected to see her at Sunday services.

WHEN JIMENA GAVE birth, her baby girl screamed.

"She's crying," the surgeon said in surprise, and said it again, "She's crying." Then two nurses in the room echoed the surgeon, yelling, "She's crying," filled with shock.

Ever rose up onto his toes to see over the curtain placed across Jimena's chest. The baby was placed inside an incubator. Her dark brown skin and outline of her body came in and out of view as a nurse took her vitals.

Jimena barked, "Ever! Go check on the baby."

She startled him and he quickly hurried over to the incubator. The nurse wiped down their baby girl, who was smaller than a doll. Her arms were short and appeared close to her body, all the joints connected but compact. Her legs were similar. Her body, too. Ever paid extra attention to her chest and saw the rise and fall.

"She's breathing!" He called back to Jimena.

She had a pudgy nose and her mouth opened wide as she let out a high-pitched and fading cry.

Ever was afraid to touch her. Not because he was afraid she might break, but because *he* might break. There was a power in her little body—almost like her skin emitted an electrical current. Slowly, he reached down and placed the tips of his fingers on her knee, and his baby girl brought tears to her father's eyes. Probably the first tears he'd cried since he was a child.

I came to understand what Ever experienced. When I

174 · Oscar Hokeah

walked into their room, I saw Jimena leaning over the
baby's incubator, Ever at her side, and I slowed my step. It
was her energy. The entire hospital room buzzed with a type
of prayer, like the air itself had been blessed by the priests.
Usually, I was like one of those tanks always firing practice
rounds at Fort Sill. But not when I stepped into that room.
It seemed like it took me an hour to walk to the edge of her
incubator.

The baby wore a tiny diaper, and her skin appeared
almost red under the lights and heat. She had tubes coming
out of her nose, and the tubes hooked up to a breathing
machine. She also had a tube through her umbilical cord,
feeding her sugar water. She would not be able to nurse or
take a bottle. There was a constant and repeated beep coming from the machine that monitored her heart. All those
wires attached to her tiny body, pobrecita, I hated to see it.

I leaned down into the incubator, laid my lips on her
forehead, gave her a kiss, and then said, "It's okay, jita, and
Mommy and Daddy are right here." I couldn't believe the
emotion that suddenly overwhelmed me. It made no sense.
She was so tiny and frail, but her energy was so powerful
it grabbed me by the heart. To stop the tears, I swallowed,
took in a deep breath, and even tried to clear my throat. I
couldn't. I started crying.

"I'm sorry," I said and quickly walked out into the
hallway.

Once outside the door, I let out a giant sob and covered

my face with my hands. There were nurses at the nurse's station nearby. I saw a window at the other end of the hall and hurried toward it. I watched cars in a parking lot below, as I cried. The ICU was four or five floors up. Buildings in downtown Oklahoma City stood in the distance. I thought of my grandparents in Mexico; somebody would have to call and tell them. I pulled out my cell phone because I needed something to stop me from crying. The tears just poured. I wiped them and they kept coming. I hadn't cried since I was a child and I'd always had a certain pride in my strength.

As soon as my grandmother was on the other end of the phone, I quickly started telling her about the baby, talking so fast I could hardly follow what was coming out of my own mouth. I didn't know what else to do with the sadness. Maybe if I rambled long enough my broken heart might unbreak.

"Como se llama?" my grandmother asked, interrupting me, getting me to stop.

"They named her after Ever's mother," I said. "Turtle Faith Geimausaddle."

"Tortuga Bebe," my abuela said.

"Jita?" she said.

"Yes, grandma."

"Ven a buscarme."

I was driving south down I-44 by the next morning. It was calming—the drive. To be honest, I had never felt so powerless. When something goes wrong with our children, we're supposed to be able to fix it. With Tortuga Bebe, there was nothing I could do. The doctors expected the machines to do more and more of her breathing. The drive gave me the illusion I was helping. I couldn't help but wonder if the breathing machine gave us the same illusion.

I drove through Texas like it wasn't even there. When I arrived at the border, the federales asked me a few questions: Where are you going? How long will you be there? Nothing major, and I didn't have to get out of my car. I told them I'd be driving back through tomorrow.

My abuelos rushed outside as I parked in their driveway. I climbed out of my SUV, and I felt as empty as the many vacant lots around Aldama. I felt like the wind cutting down one of the streets when my grandmother walked me into her house. She had a bed already made for me.

"Tienes hambre?" she asked.

I told her I wasn't hungry and I hadn't been able to eat since the day before. She placed a glass of fresh squeezed lemonade next to my bed. I downed it before falling asleep.

The next morning, my grandmother had already packed a bag with enough clothes for a week. She told me my mom could do the wash if they stayed longer. She wasn't even in Oklahoma yet and she was already bossing the family around. I suddenly saw her in me.

My father sent me a series of texts that morning, one saying, "Her oxygen levels are dropping," and another saying, "The machines are keeping her alive." Ever's family, his aunt, uncle, and cousin, were there visiting Tortuga Bebe and brought prayers. Jimena's parents had brought food and coffee for everyone, and my father texted me how he had never eaten a meal in so much silence, as everyone sat in the waiting room for their turn. Only a few visitors were allowed in the hospital room at a time. But then they allowed in a few more when too many family members built up in the waiting room.

When my abuela asked about the texts, I said, "The baby is getting a lot of visitors," and left out the rest.

We ate scrambled eggs with chorizo, which my grand-mother made in five minutes, and she was ready to go. She ushered us all out of the house and toward the SUV. It was in that moment I realized where I came from. The desert mountains around me and the cement homes surround-ing the narrow roads of Aldama swirled in my vision and seemed to almost collapse into my mind—only to unfold and spread across the Chihuahua landscape. I could see the brush of the desert in my grandmother's eyes and the harsh winds cutting through her voice. I gave my abuela a big hug.

She looked at me like I was crazy. "Date prisa y vámonos."

We drove up Chihuahua state highway 16 as the sun rose out of the east. The highway ran north but cut northeast for a large portion of the drive. For the first hour, the sun hung more to my right, but by the second hour I had to pull down my visor and sit at attention to keep the sun from cutting into my eyes. We made it to the border shortly after the sun had risen high enough to move out of my line of sight. If only sunrays in my eyes were the extent of the troubles we encountered on the drive.

Jimena had told me about her and Ever being stopped and interrogated at the border. She had never had such a hard time coming back into the U.S. before. Now we were getting the same treatment. I'd thought the Patriot Act was for terrorists, but I learned I.C.E. had something else in mind.

At the Presidio–Ojinaga Port of Entry, the line was moving much slower and there were more vehicles pulled off to the side. This was not a major entrance, not like Tijuana or El Paso. The mountains on the Mexican side kept it isolated and unpopular. So when I was asked to pull my vehicle to the side, I immediately asked, "What for?"

"Ma'am, I asked you to pull your vehicle over," the border officer said, with his thumbs tucked into the heavy black belt on his waist.

I pulled my SUV over to a building on the left and idled next to a few other vehicles. As I looked in my rearview mirror, I watched the same officer allowing vehicle after vehicle to pass, and with only a short exchange of a few words.

"They're residents going to and from work," a different officer told me. This one was taller and had more hair on his head. He walked around my SUV and inspected the wheel wells and ran a mirror underneath.

I opened my mouth to give him a piece of my mind when my grandmother grabbed my arm.

The officer made us climb out of the vehicle and forced us into a small building.

I had had enough. "I'm an American citizen. I was born here," I said.

There was a large window. Other officers were now going through my SUV, like I was a coyote. But I had nothing to hide, so I got into this officer's face.

"You don't have a right to detain me," I said. "Not only am I an American citizen but my grandparents have visas to cross back and forth. They are visiting, so what?"

The pinche pendejo wouldn't hear. Instead he forced us into a small room with only plastic chairs to sit.

Maybe it was the way I talked to the officers or maybe it was something else, but we were left in that room for two hours. Two hours. Old people can't sit in hard plastic chairs for two hours. After I complained enough, they finally moved us to a room with a small sofa. We asked for some food late in the afternoon. By dinner I had to text my father, "I don't think they're going to let us leave today."

"Please be nice to the officers, Araceli," my father texted back, as if he had been with me the whole time. But I guess he knew his daughter well. "The doctors know you're on your way. They are going to keep the machines going until you get here." Tortuga Bebe was struggling. In such a short time her health had declined to the point she couldn't breathe on her own. Machines were breathing for her. I didn't want to worry my grandparents so I stepped over to a window and kept my gaze away from them. I didn't let myself cry, but my chest tightened and I fought back the urge.

It was almost eight o'clock at night when one of the officers walked into the room and told us that my grandparents' visas were good for ten days in the United States. Who verifies anything at eight o'clock at night!? I looked at my abuela and remembered my father's request to not make trouble—so I held my breath and my words. My grandparents had dealt with enough after such a long day, so I paid for a room and we stayed the night in Presidio.

AT THE HOSPITAL, my abuela spotted Turtle right away. Me and my abuelo had to catch up to her as she hurried down the hallway toward the waiting area. She embraced Turtle and held her like a long-lost daughter, rubbing her back and holding her tight. She whispered into Turtle's ear, "Mantente fuerte" and "Va a estar bien," and Turtle thanked my grandmother for traveling all the way from Mexico.

We were a big group: my parents and grandparents, and Turtle and then Sissy and Ever's Aunt Lila, Uncle Hank, and cousin, Quinton. We all crowded into the room and found Jimena and Ever sitting next to each other on a love seat. Jimena carefully cradled the baby in her arms, trying to not disturb the tubes and wires attached to her tiny body. It was nerve-racking to hear the constant beep from the breathing machine and heart monitor.

My grandmother came to stand next to Jimena. She reached down and ran the back of her broad and textured fingers across Tortuga Bebe's check.

"Preciosa," she said. She laid her hand on Jimena's shoulder.

Jimena reached over with her free hand and took my grandmother's hand into hers.

Everyone in the room was silent. The machines beeped and beeped until the sound cut deeper into our minds than into our ears. Tortuga Bebe kept us sane as we tried to ignore the sounds. We touched her hair and her cheeks. I had to kiss her tiny toes over and over. She was so small but somehow bigger than us all.

I heard things in that hospital room my family had never said before. My abuela told Ever she was sorry her son didn't do right by him. Then Ever apologized for not showing up to his father's funeral, and Sissy said she was sorry, too. Turtle apologized to my grandparents for not making Ever and Sissy go to the funeral. My father said he had not been a good uncle to Ever, and it hit me in the heart. And then Ever apologized to my father for abandoning the family, and I suddenly wondered if we hadn't abandoned him. Then my grandparents apologized for something I thought I'd never hear them say: my tio being abusive.

For me? It happened when Ever brought in his three children to meet their baby sister. They must have only been five, four, and three years old, like stairstep triplets. One by one, they touched her cheek and kissed her forehead. Shawn asked, "When is she coming home?" and Shiloh wanted to know why there were so many tubes. Shandi's question was the hardest: "Is she okay?" The words stuck in Ever's throat, and all he could say was "I'm sorry."

Then the doctors asked for everyone to move into the waiting area. They were going to unhook Tortuga Bebe from the machines. I finally built up enough courage, and I asked Ever if we could talk. We walked to the large window at the end of the hall.

"Ever, I know how I am and what I've said to you. I just want to tell you I'm sorry."

"No, it's fine. You were right," he told me.

"I wasn't right," I said. "I make people think I'm right. I'm sorry, Cousin."

I hugged him and held him for a few seconds. My embrace couldn't fix what was happening with his baby and it couldn't fix the abuse from my tio. But I wanted it to fix what had happened between us. His hug was gentle, and I felt mine soften. My shoulders dropped and I felt his drop, too. Something lifted out of our bodies. I had pictured Ever as a monster. Did he transform? Or did I? Tortuga Bebe didn't grab anyone by the ear and force us to work things out. She drew compassion from our skin with an invisible electricity. She did more work for our families in her three days than I did in two decades.

Ever left me by the window. I watched him walk back down the hallway and disappear into the hospital room. I watched the doctors and nurses pause before the door to the room, like they were afraid to enter. Then they solemnly opened the door and stepped inside. A few minutes later, the doctors and nurses filed back out of the room. I stayed at the window. I stayed until I heard Ever cry, and then yell so loud it rolled down the hallway.

Leander Chasenuh
(2008)

I THREW A chair through the window. "I'm gonna put *your* head through it next!" I yelled.

This Pawnee kid was an OKC Crip down here on my turf. My family had started the first all-In'din gang in Lawton, and we always ran Crips out of the View. Comanches and Kiowas controlled south-side streets. I had to show him how my gang, the Rola Set, did things. The staff ran in—they must have heard the window break—and Ever stood in front of that Pawnee kid and wouldn't let me follow through with my threat.

Next thing, next day, Ever and the other staff decided I needed a little attention from the authorities; they came to talk with me about the legal consequences of physically harming other people and damaging property. Like I didn't already know. But to make it worse, Ever didn't tell me about this visit. No details, nothing. A straight-up punk move. I sat on the couch in the front office of this place they'd put me, Southern Plains Youth Development for Reoffenders. We just called it Spider. It was where they liked to put the toughest Native American kids in Oklahoma. Guess they didn't like seeing In'din kids in detention centers, but they told us the next stop was detention if Spider didn't work out. So I sat in the front office and stared out the window. Ever sat on the next couch over. A police car pulled up and parked next to the curb. That's all it took.

"They're just here to talk with you," Ever said. He stood when I stood.

"Fucking liar."

I couldn't run out the front door; I'd run straight into their hands. Instead, I ran down the hall and upstairs. The building had two floors, but the top floor only had maybe three offices, and small, too. I ran through one of the offices and saw a window. It opened out onto the roof of the first floor. I climbed out of the window and onto the roof. Ever was right behind me.

"The police are just going to talk with you."

I was sure they were going to take me to juvy.

"Leander, stop running and listen to me." He'd crawled out of the window, too, and followed me onto the roof. I ran to the edge so I could find a place to jump down, but every time I looked down, the ground was too far below.

When the two police officers crawled out the window, I panicked.

"Just come back inside and nothing is going to happen to you," Ever said. "You have my word."

But with two police officers coming up behind him, his word wasn't much. I saw an awning over a window on the second floor. It was cement. It could hold me. I would have to climb up a rain gutter and take a big step to the left. I did it in two big leaps, and then I was on top of the awning and out of everyone's reach. I squatted down and put my back against the wall, breathing deep. Ever and the police officers stood on the roof of the first floor and watched me—defeated.

At first, I visualized myself jumping down, landing on my feet, and running. I would run across the gravel parking lot. There were tall wooden fences, but I could jump them. I had jumped those kinds of fences before. And once I got past the fences, there would be no way Ever and those pigs-in-a-blanket could catch me. But the distance to the ground looked like a million miles.

As I stared at the gravel rocks below, I was suddenly confused. I'm on an awning, I thought, and for a moment I wondered why. The literal thought of "How did I get here?" suddenly became more abstract.

WHAT DO I remember the most about my mom? Her perfume. My mother was a Chasenuh. The last time I seen her I was five years old, maybe six. I sat on a pillow in the front seat of her car. It was late at night. There were headlights passing as we drove somewhere—I don't remember where. I do remember how I liked to sit on the pillow, so I could see out the front window. The smell of hard liquor filled the car and not because my mother was drinking, but because it radiated through her pores. For the longest time I thought the smell of liquor was her perfume. That night, I saw the shadow of a man walking on the side of the road and then the front of our car slam into him. His body went down. Two hard knocks underneath my seat. The car bounced and swerved. My mother pulled the car under control and kept driving, her eyes wide like her mouth. I jerked backward in my seat when she slammed her foot on the gas.

After my mother went to prison, but before my father was locked up, he made me stay outside. Most of the time I was in the alleys. I followed stray dogs from trash can to trash can. People threw away full packages of hot dogs or half-eaten pizzas. Those mutts taught me how to eat good on the streets. You know how a dog can growl deep in its throat? I can do that to this day. I have to catch myself from biting at someone's hair if they're close to me. Those mangy little mutts kept me alive. When it was cold out, I'd pound on the door to my house, howling at my dad and barking. He'd open the door just to get me to shut up. I'm not sure how long this went on—maybe a year or longer—it was a while in my memory. I do remember the day when a neighbor lady—she was a Tahsequah—came over and took me to her house and cooked me a hot meal. I threw it up because I had never eaten a hot meal before.

In the summer, Dad locked me out overnight. You know that bad kid running up and down the roads, getting into people's stuff? That was me. The older kids laughed when I'd cuss them out. They'd get me high and drunk and watch me act a fool, a little guy staggering around and trying to fight. They taught me a street game the Rola Set called Name Echoes Name. You'd have to yell out your last name into the neighborhoods. "Make everyone in the View hear it," they told me, "Whoever doesn't say their name gets an ass kicking." As soon as someone said, "Name echoes name!" I'd yell out "Chasenuh!" in my little voice and puff my chest out, arms wide, ready to get jumped. This was my first introduction to the Rola Set, and I got jumped in when I was ten years old, a few days after they took my dad to prison.

SITTING ON THE awning, I looked over at Ever and those two police officers and I wondered what kind of childhood they had. Instead of jumping to run, I wanted to jump to die. It wasn't going to get better, only worse. Why live?

Ever kept asking me to climb down. He stood at the edge of the roof with his hand out, said, "Let me help you."

"You're not going to die if you jump," one of the police officers said. As if in unison, the other officer finished the first one's thought, and added, "You're just going to fuck yourself up real good." The first officer picked up right after, and said, "If you don't come down on your own then I'm going to shoot you with a Taser and you'll just fall off and break something," and the second officer added (as if they had rehearsed this skit a million times), "Either way works for us."

I dropped my head in defeat and then looked over at Ever. His hand was out. He could have easily fallen off the way he leaned, with a foot propped on the edge of the roof. The way I remember it he had watery eyes, but maybe that's just my memory. Ever's a tough guy with broad shoulders and grew up on the same streets as me. I can't imagine him getting emotional. Even still, I'm going to remember him with tears in his eyes. "Come on, Leander," he told me, "I got you." I let out a deep growl with a slow breath and grabbed his hand.

I spent two weeks in a mental hospital before they let me see Ever again. He was the one who drove the van from the group home to pick me up. Man, I was so happy to see him, and happy to get out of that nuthouse. The first thing I said to him was, "Why'd you leave me in there with all those crazy people?" And he laughed.

"IF YOU COME to live in my home, you have to do *one* thing for me," Ever told me, "When you start to get pissed, I want you to draw."

The group home lost its main source of funding. Spider had some kind of contract with the feds to work with In'din kids who committed crimes on federal land, which means In'din land. They had a group home, but also foster homes for violent kids. The way I looked at it, Spider shutting down its group home was a good thing because I got to go to Therapeutic Foster Care with Ever. A lot of those kids, though, had to go to a detention center. Ever was the only staff who chose to stay on with Spider and take me as a foster kid. We wore staff out like new erasers on drawing paper—quick and without remorse.

He told me all I needed was a home and a family and I would make better choices. He liked to say, "Small expectations rise like water in a canal." He wanted me to be a part of his household, like it was made of magic or something. I didn't think there was anything, magic or not, that could get me to stop feeling like this. Four walls were just walls, no matter where I slept—a detention, a group home, an apartment—it was all the same to me. I didn't give a shit.

Ever was so sure there was a difference between four walls and a home.

"Is it a deal?" he asked.

I didn't want to go to no detention center, so I said, "Deal."

WE WERE DRIVING up Sheridan Avenue at night, with headlights passing by. It had been a little over a week since I moved into his apartment. Ever handed me a drawing pad and a pencil. I took the pencil and clenched it in my fist like a knife.

"What would you do if I stabbed you in the neck with this?" I said.

He had just picked me up from the Teen Center and we were headed to his house on the North Side. His three kids were in the back seat. Normally, his wife had the kids, but she was out. He had two sons and one daughter, eight, seven, and six years old. The daughter was the youngest. His wife took care of those kids like they were her own, but they weren't even her kids. They had lost a baby after it was born, and maybe this was the reason she was so close to his kids. But Kiowas and Comanches all had adopted relatives. And Ever taking me, a Comanche, into his Kiowa family was like that. He was always trying to show me I was a part of his family. And tonight, he had all of us.

"I'm not going to do anything," he said, "because you're *not* going to stab me with that pencil."

"How do you know?" I asked him, with the pencil in my hands. "You don't know me. My dad and uncles did home invasions. It's in my blood to stab people."

"Draw me one of those lowriders," he said. "I like the Monte Carlos on three-wheel motion."

I turned the pencil around in my hand and drew "Rola Set" in graffiti-style letters. I lifted the paper and showed him. He pointed at the empty space beneath the letters. "You can draw that Monte right there."

I said, "fuck you," under my breath and then went to drawing a Monte Carlo. He never made a big deal about what I drew. When I was in the group home, the other staff would get pissed off when I'd draw some gang reference or a half-naked woman, but Ever told me to draw whatever I wanted. He had this wall in his bedroom, when you opened his bedroom door, where he'd taped up my pictures. Only the appropriate ones, though. He had about a dozen Monte Carlos from different angles, but I also liked to draw roses, smile-now-cry-later faces, and hearts with a vine filled with thorns across it. Ever called it prison art, and he was right because they were drawn on the letters my father sent me from inside the pen. I liked to copy them. I also liked to draw the Lil Homies collection. On the first day I moved into his apartment, he took me to Hobby Lobby and we bought around twenty drawing pads and ten boxes of drawing pencils. He'd placed a drawing pad and pencil in every room of the apartment and he placed two in the car, one in the front seat and one in the back.

IT WAS ASSAULT and battery, if you're wondering why I had to go to Spider in the first place. One night I drank too much and started snorting coke. I was only fourteen and it was my first time doing coke. Five members of a gang called Vice Lords decided to roll through our neighborhood that night. I beat all five, knocked one guy unconscious with a tree limb, but I kept beating him with that limb until he woke back up and ran away with a bloody head. The police tased and hog-tied me. I turned fifteen inside Spider, and soon after moving into Ever's place I turned sixteen. When I told Ever that I wanted to go to high school like a normal kid, he laughed at me. Then he apologized.

"With your record," he said, "I don't think any school is going to let you in."

It was true, I didn't have the best behavior in schools either. In fact, I hadn't been in a normal school since the sixth grade. I had gotten suspended every year in elementary for fighting, but then in sixth grade I told some kid that I was going to bring a gun to school. I wasn't going to shoot the school up like you see on the news. When I got pissed I made threats or fought someone. I told this guy at school that I would bring a gun to school and put it in his face and then we'd see how tough he was. Someone told a teacher. Next thing I knew, the police escorted me off school grounds. I was expelled over that. The way things were—with a school shooting every week in the U.S.—it was zero tolerance.

Despite all those odds Ever set up a meeting to see if I could attend Eisenhower High. We met in a big room at the school. I sat at one end of this long table and there were at least nine other people there along with Ever, my social worker, and my parole officer. There were two school counselors, the principal, vice principal, and three other people who said they were from a school board. I felt like the main course at an all-you-can-eat buffet. They had copies of everything: my school attendance record, behavior record, and transcripts, probably more, too, because I had been in special needs schools since the sixth grade incident.

"Why should I let you into my school?" the principal asked. She had hair the color of a rusted car bumper. I opened my mouth, but nothing came out. Ever tried to answer for me, but the principal said, "No, I'd like to hear this directly from Leander."

"Because I'm ready to make changes," I said. Ever looked at me. We were both shocked at what came out of my mouth. Maybe I was more shocked than he was, because those words were real. "I'm living with Ever and his family. I made a deal with him and I'm doing good with sticking to it."

"What's the deal?" one of the school counselors asked.

"When I get mad, I draw," I said. I pulled out a picture that I drew to show everyone at the table. I didn't tell Ever that I was going to bring the picture. I had worked on this drawing the day before and I'd finished it that morning. It was the canal that ran through the middle of Mattie Beal Park. After a heavy spring rain, the canal filled all the way up to its banks, about fifteen feet high. The Lawton canals were big because the rains on the Southern Plains could easily flood the city and often did. On one side of the canal there were these large stones that were around four foot high and just as wide. A young man sat on one of those large rocks in his baggy jeans. He had a long ponytail. He sat looking across the canal. On the other side of the flowing water were a group of In'din men in their thirties and forties sitting in a circle next to a large cottonwood tree. One In'din man was walking up to the circle of men. He had a thick, long stick in his hand, and he was in mid-swing as he aimed it at the side of one man's head. That was the last time I saw my father, swinging a stick at a man's head while I sat across the canal. The only thing in the drawing that wasn't true to that day was the water in the canal. I put that in myself. After my father hit the man on the side of the head, I immediately jumped off that rock and walked toward the road, heading back to the View.

"You're very good at drawing," the vice principal said.

I shrugged my shoulders. "I draw what I don't want to be."

Later, Ever asked me about the drawing. I told him, "I don't want to be like my dad."

Ever told me how a Cherokee mask had helped him overcome the fear of his father. The mask hung on his living room wall. I'd noticed it but never said anything. It kind of spooked me to ask other In'dins about ceremonial stuff. We were taught to never ask. When it was time to know, then elders would explain. Until then? Never ask. Ever told me how his uncle gave him the booger mask to help him overcome his fear of his father's abuse.

"If we were echoes from one voice we wouldn't carry very far," he said. "We've echoed through endless generations because we are constructed by the voices of many."

I think of Ever telling me that when I remember the canal picture I drew.

That day, the counselor had a few questions for me and so did the three from the school board. By the end of the meeting everyone had looked at my drawing. They all decided that I should get a second chance. "Everyone deserves second chances," the principal said, with the drawing in her hands, "but if you mess up even once then you're out. Do you understand me, Leander?"

I nodded. I looked over at Ever and he had a smile on his face bigger than mine.

THERE WASN'T A day that went by that I didn't get pissed off. Every time Ever would hand me a drawing pad and pencil, and asked, "Do you want to draw for a little while?" I took the pad mostly because of the deal I made with him—not because I wanted to. But I made friends at school. I got my own backpack and had books to carry, like a normal kid. I'm not going to say that I didn't put a couple holes in my bedroom wall, or I didn't cuss at Ever. But I did hold things together well enough to attend regular high school for over a month. When I earned the privilege to attend a football game, I smoked a little weed, thinking no one would find out. Besides, I was a street kid going to school with a bunch of punk-ass bitches. I thought the weed might chill me out, but this kid mocked me, saying, "Check out this real *gangster*," exaggerating "gangster" with a nerdy voice. So I popped him in the mouth. I had to show ol' boy what real "gangsters" did. We were in a big group, and a teacher confronted me and could smell the marijuana, and then a security guard escorted me off the premises. Ever picked me up, and he could smell the weed on me, too.

TWO DAYS LATER, I had eggs going on the stove. I asked for a knife so I could cut open a package of bacon. The knives were behind two locks in his house since he had to hold to the same protocol as a group home. All that stuff—meds, sharps, cleaners—were locked up. He went and got the knife and handed it to me and I cut open the package of bacon.

"Do you think my eggs look alright?" I asked.

He glanced over. "Yeah. They look good."

"You didn't even look at them. They look like shit, huh?"

"Leander, they are good," he said, this time giving the eggs a good look.

I grabbed the knife—I'm not sure why—and I held it in my hands at my side like I wanted to use it on him.

"Put the knife down," he said.

"Are you going to make me?"

"No. Let's put it down and we'll sit down and draw something," Ever said. He reached over to the counter, where a pad and a couple of pencils sat. "Let's trade. You give me the knife, and I'll give you these."

"Fuck you, you're lying to me. I cook like shit," I said. "You draw something, if you like pictures so goddamn much."

"Leander, give me the knife."

"You're such a fucking liar."

"We're going to find you another school," he said, "it's one setback, Leander. We've been through worse. We'll get through this one, too."

I stood there, inches from his face, the knife clenched down at my side. I stepped over to the counter and slammed the knife down on the counter and went back to the package of bacon. Ever grabbed the knife. He wiped it off and then put it inside a lockbox and locked the lockbox inside a kitchen closet. I grabbed a fistful of bacon strips from the package and slammed them into the pan. I cooked the rest of my breakfast so agitated I wanted to punch the wall.

THE ONLY THING that kept me from putting myself back into detention was the local Teen Center. I was allowed to go between noon and three because that's when the other kids were in school. I was around adult staff for three hours, but they were cool and I could play video games, lift weights, play basketball, get on the computer, or play pool.

A few months later, Ever found me a volunteer job for a Boys & Girls Club. He pulled some strings. And he set up some rules, like zero tolerance and I had to have an adult staffer with me at all times. He put his reputation on the line. My job was to help elementary school kids with their homework after school. They'd all arrive at the Club after three, on buses. Sometimes we played dodgeball or basketball after all the homework was done. After being there for a few weeks, I started to teach a few of the kids how to draw. I liked the aggressive kids. They made me laugh with some of the things they would say. I taught them how to draw lowriders and smile-now-cry-later faces. After about a month of teaching drawing on the side, the director of the Club caught wind of it and she made it an official class, my art class.

My peers at the Club were my age but they weren't kids from the ghetto. Most of them were white. These teens were overachievers, talked about getting mad about a *B* in a class, or argued with each other about which was better: University of Oklahoma or Oklahoma State. Teens with aspirations were freaks to me. They actually wanted to be leaders in the community. At first, I'd tell them to shut up if they even walked up to me. They reminded me of the kid I popped in the mouth at the high school. But then they complimented my drawing, and a few of them joined my class. They were afraid of me and they didn't talk shit. I liked that. After a while, I started to check myself on a lot of things, like my language and talking about thugging. It was different, but I wanted to be a good influence.

And Ever had found a GED class for me. I went from GED class, to the Teen Center, and then to the Boys & Girls Club every day. I hung out with Ever and his family on the weekends. If we weren't at the powwows, then we'd be at the gym or a park.

Something happened, though.

Still, every day, it seemed, I woke up hardcore angry. I don't know why. One morning, we were running late for my GED class. Ever barked at me a few times, rushing me, and I got agitated. I was trying to hold in all my anger. That morning we climbed into Ever's car, I wanted to blast him in the face. I clenched my fist, and I started to growl like those mangy stray dogs running down the alleys. I tapped my knuckles on the dash. I wanted to slam my fist into the windshield and splinter it. I'd watched my father do that once. I visualized, clearly, my knuckles banging into the glass and the glass cracking under the force, and my knuckles filling with blood. If I could do that to a window, I thought: What could I do to Ever's face?

He snapped at me, "You take too long," as he sped out of the apartment parking lot.

I reached into the side pocket on the door and pulled out a pencil. I gripped it to stab him in the throat. I visualized that, too. How the car would swerve and crash. How I'd get out of the car and run.

I looked at Ever's face, his long black hair in a tight pony-tail. Suddenly, I couldn't remember what my own father looked like. Did he look like Ever? Why did I care? Did it really fucking matter anymore? Ever was the one rushing to get me to school on time. He was stressing out to help me. He showed up every day, rain or shine, good or bad. I reached back over to the side pocket and pulled out a pad. I quickly made myself draw.

I suppose Ever was right about small expectations: they rise like water.

Opbee Geimausaddle
(2010)

BUH, ALL THOSE years, and I thought Lena was Kiowa. Didn't even find out until last year at her funeral. The preacher pulled me aside and asked, "Opbee, do you know Lena's clan?" I made a face, slapped him in the arm, like he was joshing, because Kiowas didn't have clans. Then he went and told me Lena was Cherokee. Ah'guh! Here I thought she was Gkoi all my life. Uncle Vincent had first brought her around when I was just an ankle biter. I must have been ten or eleven years old at the time. This was before they had any kids. Uncle Vincent and Aunt Lena would travel from Lawton to Carnegie for family visits. Once they had

Lila they visited less, and then after Turtle they hardly came around. I always remembered Lena because of the quilt she gave me. Then I saw Ever at the gourd dance selling quilts. Made me think of his grandmother, Lena.

I watched Hank Quoetone spread a Pendleton on the floor in the middle of the powwow arena—not too far from the singers. I thought the Societies were honoring the drum, taking up a collection. I think it was Sizzortail, or maybe Rocky Boys—we invited singers from different parts so it was hard to say. But it turned out that the blanket wasn't for the drum. It was for my nephew, Ever, his three littles, and his adopted son, Leander. Leander worked over in Lawton at the tire plant, so he wasn't there that day.

I had never met Ever before, even though he was my nah'ee. He was a nephew through my cousin, Turtle, who I hardly knew. Uncle Vincent had relocated to Lawton, after he served in the Korean War, to find a job. There wasn't much work in Carnegie, so Kiowas often moved to Lawton or Anadarko or Oklahoma City.

It surprised me to see Ever at the powwow. He had our family's distinctive look, with arms long enough to reach the top of a roof. I couldn't help but think of his momma, the way the corners of his mouth turned downward with sharp lines. But I suppose all us Geimausaddles had this similarity. Ever led his kids into the arena, and they walked behind him from oldest to youngest, like a family of ducks crossing a busy road. They came to stand behind the Pendleton blanket. Shawn was ten and the oldest. He took after my Uncle Vincent something fierce. Then there was Shiloh: nine and built broad like his Cherokee side. Shandi crawled into my heart as soon as I saw those pigtails. She was eight but had a younger spirit about her.

Hank Quoetone had the microphone in his hand and he announced, "I'm calling for a blanket dance. This is for my nephew, Ever Geimausaddle, and his kids. The company he worked for lost all of its funding so he was laid off, and his car was repossessed. He's having a hard time getting his kids to and from school. We're asking for any help you can offer."

An elder Botone handed Ever a gourd rattle. Then I saw Hank's wife, my cousin Lila, carrying a Gourd Club shawl, baby blue, into the arena and heading for Shandi. The shawl was too big so Lila folded it in half. Shandi struggled to hold the large shawl over her shoulders, shifting this way and that, the way littles did. None of them had any regalia, they wore jeans and T-shirts. All four stood alongside the blanket waiting for the drummers to start the song.

I've seen many blanket dances in my day, growing up Gkoi, but there was something especially heartbreaking about a single parent down on their luck. Many of us, most of us, could see ourselves in Ever, like we had either been where he was or feared we'd end up there. We were taught to give or else more would be taken. Streams of people walked into the arena, while drumbeats and voices filled

Red Buffalo Hall. We crumpled bills in our hands and tossed them onto the blanket. We stood next to Ever and his three kids and danced alongside. Must have been a good thirty people out there. The line of people made a half circle around the drum. Ever and his kids stood to one side with the Pendleton blanket spread in front of them. Some gourd dancers moved through the arena, while the singers' heavy and low voices carried through our bodies. We danced, the way Kiowas danced, when called by our people, by our ancestors, to help each other heal.

"*Whiiitchaa!*" Hank Quoetone yelled into the microphone. "So beautiful!"

All the dancers dipped a little lower and rose a little higher to the drumbeat, and the singers prayed for our spirits, calling for our ancestors.

"Step into the arena! Dance with us! Honor this young man and his children!"

By the time the song was finished, the blanket was filled from edge to edge with crumpled dollar bills. And we were filled with a renewed energy. Sometimes a blanket dance can fill up your spirit, and this was one of those moments. I'll never forget it. A gift.

Afterward, I saw Ever walking around the arena with a large bag of quilts, selling them off. In my day, quilts had been a big deal. A great quilter in the family quickly became ah'day, special, honored. I watched Ever shake everyone's hand, the custom after a blanket dance or honor song, but I kept a close eye on those quilts. I couldn't help but remember his grandmother, Lena, and the quilt she'd given me. I sat with my family and watched as he made his way around the arena. I wondered if Lena had made the ones he was selling. But I lost sight of him when one of my nieces asked me to fix the leather wraps in her braids.

Ever caught my eye again a few moments later when an elder Botone handed him some money. He pulled the quilts out of the bag and examined them. From the stack, it seemed like there were four. They all had the same design, bird patterns in corresponding squares, but each quilt had its own color scheme. As the elder considered each, I focused on the violet and mauve one, which, luckily, he didn't buy.

I thought about buying one of those quilts, too, but before I decided Ever had already left the gourd dance. Lila said he'd taken Hank's car to pick up Leander from his shift at Goodyear. I asked her about the quilts.

"When I see Ever later I'll ask him to save one for you, Opbee," she said.

I didn't have patience to wait and had to see for myself. I looked around the arena at all those faces. It was antsville. Must have been a couple hundred people. The elder who bought the quilt wasn't a big guy, kind of scrawny, but he was easy to spot because he wore Kiowa colors on his regalia. Soon enough I found him at the snack bar buying a few bottles of water. Might know, he was the son to one of my older cousins, Geimausaddle'daw, so he was a relative and about my same age.

"Hey, aw'thaw, would you mind if I looked at that quilt you bought?" I asked. I just wanted to take a closer look at the design.

I loved the bird patterns repeated across the fabric, like a family perched in a tree, and the navy blue and canary yellow offset each other well. I liked how the dark and light contrasted. But what most interested me was the stitch, white thread, that ran in arches from each corner until all four cascading stitches met in the center. I ran my fingers over the thread and saw it was hand sewn. The stitches were all different lengths, as someone had carefully pulled a needle down and then back up through the fabric. It was beautiful, and a quality I just didn't see very often. More important, the stitch was familiar. I had seen it somewhere before.

"You take it, naw'thaw," my relative told me. "You seem to know more about it than I do."

At first I refused, but we're not supposed to turn down a gift.

I held the quilt in my lap for a little while. Relatives were up and down out of their seats, as they went to dance or were called into the arena. I tried to hold my enthusiasm, like holding onto the edges of my shawl when I danced. But I suppose my knees did ache. Maybe it was best to go home early anyway, I told myself. Then I made excuses about leaving the powwow early.

"My arthritis is acting up," I told them.

They grinned after glancing at the quilt in my arms. Guess my excitement showed more than I realized.

After racing home, I went straight to my bedroom. I tossed the new quilt onto the bed and pulled out the old quilt—the one Lena stitched—from my closet. I unfolded it. The blue-gray fabric triggered a gust of memories, like when I opened my windows for the first time in spring and cool air washed over me. I had come across this quilt several times, looking through my other blankets, but I hadn't unfolded it in years. I knew it was over fifty years old, so I didn't want to put any more wear on it than needed. A part of me worried it would crumble under my fingers. I laid my hand on it for a moment and slid my palm across. The fabric had faded. It was more gray than blue. And the accents were a faded maroon.

I lay the quilts beside each other on my bed. Ever's was cherry, so vibrant the colors popped. Mine was dull and faded because it was so old. I wanted to inspect the stitches alongside each other. Just to make certain. And, sure enough, it was as I suspected. The white thread ran in a series of arches, like multiple rainbow shapes from each corner—until the arches met in the center of the quilt. I laid my hand on my chest and couldn't believe. Lena must have made this quilt shortly before she passed away. One of her last. The fabric appeared to be crisp to the touch, and the colors were so bright the patterns almost seemed to hover.

Something caught my eye. There was a small embroidered piece in the bottom corner of Ever's quilt. The thread was navy blue and bright enough to notice. I had to pull the corner up to my face to read the lettering: Leander.

I paused, and suddenly noticed I had stopped breathing. I snapped myself out.

I quickly grabbed the other quilt—my quilt—and pulled up each corner. The first, nothing, the second, nothing, and the third corner the same as the other two. It was in the last corner I found something I must have forgotten. It was a small embroidered accent in faded blue-gray thread spelling my name: Opbee.

IT WAS SO long ago, but the memories came flooding back. As soon as my parents went splitsville, my mother went mon'sape. Just like that. All of a sudden. Zadle'bay! Then my poor father had double the chores and half the time. There he was, scrambling with two hands to juggle what had been done with four. Worse still, he had three angry daughters because our mother was suddenly gone. We should've been mad at her. Might know, everything became Dad's fault. When he didn't cook dinner fast enough, when he was late dropping us off at school, when he didn't have the energy for our homework. I made a fuss when he put my hair into the same clumpy ponytail every day. How he didn't take us to the park on the weekends and how he stopped taking us to the gourd dances. One ball hit another, and my father was getting hit from four different directions.

My youngest sister slammed the doors in the house; my middle sister pushed me off the porch; but I just tended to do things to myself so that no one could see. My father never knew about the bite marks on my arm. But I couldn't control the night terrors. I woke from nightmares yelling for my mother, and everything started to scare me, especially dark places like the bedroom closet or underneath my bed. I heard voices—loud and scary—telling me things like "I hate you" and "hurt yourself" or "run away." Month after month, I woke in the night complaining of a stomachache, only to crawl into bed with my father. Eventually he told me, "Opbee, you're half my size and take up twice as much bed."

Then Uncle Vincent stopped by to visit one Saturday afternoon with his new wife, Lena, and they sat with my dad at the kitchen table, drinking coffee. My dad told them about the divorce, my mother, how she never visited. He told on each of us. Sure enough, he told Uncle Vincent and Aunt Lena about my night terrors. But his voice slowed. In my case, he wasn't venting about being a single parent. He was concerned. He told how I climbed into his bed every night and complained of stomachaches.

"I might have to take her to be blessed by the medicine bundles," he said.

Lena turned to me. "Opbee, did you know I make magic quilts?"

My mind went to flying quilts or quilts turned into a portal, carrying me into another world, even for a moment, to forget how my mother didn't love me anymore. My eyes lit up when she said, "I'm going to bring you one." She said that they had the power to chase away monsters in the night, and mostly, they could cure sick bellies.

The following Saturday, Dad told me that Uncle Vincent and Aunt Lena would be driving up from Lawton. I was so excited I sat on the front porch for what felt like hours, even though it was just a thirty-minute drive. Here I thought it took them half the day. Each minute passed like those old metal pumps sucking oil out of the Southern Plains, screechingly painful. When Uncle Vincent's Apache truck pulled into the driveway, I raced over to Aunt Lena's side of the truck. I was pressed so close to the truck that she said, "Opbee, let me open my door, babe."

She held the quilt in her arms. It was blue-gray with maroon diamond shapes. I walked alongside her to the house, reaching out to run my hand across the fabric. I must've smiled like a pond turtle, I was so excited. Everyone gathered in the living room, my father and sisters, while Lena unfolded the quilt. The blue-gray background had a shimmering tint to it and made the maroon diamonds filling the center appear as though they were floating. I'm sure I squealed because I always squealed, and to be honest I'm known to squeal even to this day.

Lena came down to one knee and looked at me. "You have to take good care of it. This is a very powerful quilt."

She told me how I had to be tucked in every night with a special series of tasks. My dad had to tell me a Saynday story, too. Then she lifted a corner of the quilt and showed me my embroidered name.

SEEING THAT EMBROIDERY that afternoon lifted me into a gust of memories, like I was a young mau'tawn again, like the first time I wrapped Lena's quilt around my body. It energized me. For an old lady like myself, those energizing moments were few and far between. I couldn't help but want more, to know more, and mostly to give back to Lena by way of her grandson Ever, but her great grandchildren, too. I wanted to provide her littles with the same comfort Lena gave me all those years ago. I hated to think about them babies being without their quilts. Every night crawling into their beds, wondering. I just couldn't stand the thought. I had to track down those quilts. I could already see the look on their faces when I handed each back to them.

Being Gkoi was like everyone was born from the same womb, tightly knit, so families weren't hard to find. All I needed were last names. Too, I had an advantage, because the Quoetones were one of those families who had a relative in every Society. My cousin, Lila, probably married Hank Quoetone because she was made from the same quilt. They both had friends around every corner. Their son, Quinton, ran security at all the powwows. Collectively they knew just about everyone in southern Oklahoma. All it took was a call. Lila asked Hank, who said Quinton ran security at the Tahhahwah benefit powwow, and Quinton told her that a Tahhahwah had bought one of Ever's quilts.

I had to find out if they were the Lawton Tahhahwahs or the ones who moved south to the town of Walters. I called Linda Tahhahwah, who said that the benefit powwow had been for her niece, Renee. She was going to OU in the fall, and they had raised money for sheets, blankets, towels, and all the items a college student might need. I asked her about Ever and she knew Ever by his oldest boy, Shawn Geimausaddle.

"Shawn lost a stepmother, Jimena, through a divorce," she told me, and added, "Shawn is a special boy." My first thought? Ah'day. But Shawn had adapted the best, or better than his two younger siblings, because he took on Leander's attitude, who had already lost both his biological parents to incarceration. It was Leander who heard Ever and Jimena yelling at each other. He had his bags packed before the argument was over, and he helped his siblings round up their things: Shawn didn't want to forget his basketball, Shiloh needed his MP3 player with all his music, and Shandi packed most of her suitcase with her Littlest Pet Shop toys, holding the Pet Shop bus under her arm. It was Leander who loaded all three kids into the car.

After my nah'ee and Jimena lost their first child years ago, Leander quickly became like a son to Ever. But Jimena wanted to have children of her own. Too, they already had four, Ever thought, and that was enough. She was six years younger, Jimena, in her mid-twenties, and dreamed of starting her own tribe; four was no different than five, six, or more. Those dreams must've meant more to her than Ever recognized. Before either truly understood how losing a child might affect their marriage, they were divorced.

Haw, Ever moved all his kids into a three-bedroom trailer in the View. Most people avoided the south side of Lawton; it was notorious for gangs and crime. But Ever had only been working part-time with the after-school program at Roosevelt Elementary School. Too, his aunt and uncle's garage wasn't a large enough space for him and the kids. The trailer in the middle of the View was all he could afford. Linda told me Leander had his own room, Shawn and Shiloh shared a room, and Shandi had her own room. Ever slept on the couch in the living room. He often found his neighbor, a young white lady, asleep on his front lawn. She had problems with meth and alcohol—sop'ho—too many in Oklahoma were that way. But it was that kind of neighborhood.

Ever didn't want to sign up on the waiting list for an Indian Home through the Kiowa Tribe. He said Carnegie, Gotebo, and Mount View were too far away from work. He could've looked for a job in 'Darko or Chickasha. But it was the same difference; he knew he needed to settle his kids into a better place, a place he could call his own. He was at a point where placing one foot in front of the other used most of his energy. A trailer home inside the View was one step, piecing together work was another, helping his kids survive divorce was a big step, and then the absence of a mother figure was more like a supernatural leap. It was like jumping over the whole of Lake Latonka and then facing Mount Scott afterward.

Ever's first challenge came with Shawn nearly slipping away. But Shawn had a resilience about him that came from his great grandfather, my Uncle Vincent's natural gift for athleticism. Many ta'lees like Shawn used sports, like basketball, to survive. And it helped that he was tall and lanky. But what made him good at basketball wasn't my Uncle Vincent's genetics. It was rage. He threw elbows like a dog soldier staked to the ground, fighting for his life. He knocked down teens twice his size, and dribbled the ball between people like he was dodging arrows aimed at his heart. Shawn would go to the park right after school and not come home until well after dark, playing by the streetlights in game after game.

Shawn Geimausaddle had met Linda and Bobby Tahhahwah shortly after Ever moved into the View. Their son Anthony played on the same basketball team. The boys went to the same school, Roosevelt Elementary. Bobby had gotten Anthony in a number of basketball leagues playing against teams as far north as Oklahoma City. Bobby asked if Shawn could tag along. "Your boy's as fierce as the sun," he told Ever.

Call them the son of the sun split in half. Might know, Shawn and Anthony were like Half Boys, traveling together to a different town every night. They'd play a game in Chickasha on Monday and then they'd be in Anadarko on Tuesday and end up in Duncan by Wednesday. Too, the weekends had them moving nonstop, so Shawn slept overnights at Anthony's house through Sunday. "I told my husband he needed to back off," Linda said later. Shawn and Anthony would learn new basketball moves together, studying video recordings of their games, and throwing no-look basketball passes like they were psychic. Sure enough, they won five games in a row. Bobby took them out to eat and bought them new basketball gear. After ten games in a row, he took them to watch a new NBA team called the Oklahoma City Thunder. The boys shook Kevin Durant's hand and received a signed basketball card. Between three different basketball Little Leagues and games through Roosevelt, the boys won twenty straight games together. Bobby thought he had a pair of ah'days.

"You have your hands full with all your kids," Bobby told Ever when he dropped Shawn off after another winning weekend of games. "It'll take time to get back on your feet. If you're in a bind, we'd be happy to adopt Shawn. We love him like a son."

Kiowas and Comanches have a lot of similarities, one being our love for adoption. We'll adopt just about anybody. But haw'nay, Ever didn't like the idea of someone trying to adopt his son. First he pulled Shawn out of the leagues on the weekends and told Bobby, "We have family responsibilities with the Societies." The Tahhawahs had relatives involved with Comanche Little Ponies and Comanche War Scouts, so Linda and Bobby couldn't argue against it. "Culture before basketball," Ever told them, and might know Shawn no longer spent weekends with the Tahhahwahs.

Ever had his cousin Quinton take over with Shawn's practices. Shawn already had a family, and Ever meant to send Bobby that message loud and clear.

It all weighed heavy on Linda's heart. She said, "If you see Ever, can you apologize to him for me and my husband? Bobby was a little too excited and wasn't trying to offend."

It was Linda's sister Angela who bought a red-and-gray quilt from Ever. It was a gift for Linda's niece, Renee. Sure enough, Angela was part of the Tahhahwahs who moved south to Walters. Linda gave me her number and I called to ask if I could see her, and might know Angela's voice was so similar it was like talking to Linda all over again.

I drove to Walters the same afternoon and asked as politely as possible, "Would you consider selling me the quilt?"

It surprised me when Angela paused, falling silent for a moment. Then she said something about the quilt: it had OU colors. The red was dark enough to be crimson, and often cream was replaced with gray. Renee was attending OU in the fall, and sure enough, the going-away party was set for early August. Too, the quilt was the big gift from the family.

"Can I show you something on there?" I asked her. I was a little ahead of myself. To be honest, I wasn't sure if it was even going to be there. Was it the same stock as mine and Leander's? Angela led me to her bedroom and started digging in her closet. She pulled out the quilt, letting it unfold in her arms. The maroon on white was crisp and bright. I even gasped a little, and my breath caught in my throat. I ran a hand over the fabric while Angela held it in her arms. She laid the quilt onto her bed. I immediately went to the corners. From one to the other, I lifted the edges of the quilt. Then I stopped when I found what I was looking for, what I was hoping for. I showed Angela the red embroidery: Shawn.

I told my own story, Geimausaddle-daw, but more important my connection to Ever's grandmother, Lena: Shawn's own opbee, his "big sister"—great-grandmother. Shawn needed his opbee's quilt, and it would go a long way toward healing the family. Angela folded the quilt and then held it out to me. I pulled out $1,000 in cash that I'd gotten out of the bank, ready to pay her.

"No," she said and turned my hand away. "This is a gift."

THAT NIGHT, I called Hank Quoetone to find out where the other quilts had gone. He remembered seeing Ever sell one at the Kiowa–Apache Blackfoot Society's annual pow-wow. And of course the first person I thought of was Brenda Redbone. She was a Kiowa War Mother and worked at the Apache complex. I asked to take her to lunch, so we met at

Mazzio's Pizza over in 'Darko. Her son, Ronnie, who was the same age as my daughter, was a part of the Blackfoot Society. Brenda really pulled out one of those flip phones—all fancy—right there in the middle of Mazzio's and called Ronnie.

Sure enough Ronnie had been at the benefit a few weeks back and he said, "There was a Geimasauddle who had a blanket dance."

"Yeah, that's my nah'ee," I told Brenda from across the table. "Does he know who bought the quilt?"

"Who bought it?" she yelled into the flip phone. Then she paused and suddenly her face contorted, and said, "No, not the rims on your truck," and laughed at him; then yelled, "A quilt! Ever Geimasauddle sold a quilt that night. Who bought it?"

Brenda didn't even say goodbye. Buh! She just flipped the phone shut. She huffed and took a drink of Pepsi. Then she turned to me and said, "Some Kiowa from Gotebo bought it. He said it was a Kopepassah." Call me a typical Kiowa, but I immediately thought of my relatives. It was a small Kiowa world since lineage and honor had us connecting relations from both sides of the family. "Bilateral descent" was how academics described us. "Family people" was how we described ourselves. My aunt's husband's cousin, Simon Kopepassah, was always at the powwows, so I knew he'd bought that quilt.

Maybe two hours later, I pulled into Simon's driveway. It was past Carnegie way, somewhere around Mount View. So far out onto the Southern Plains I almost fell asleep driving. Didn't help that I had big bote after eating all that pizza. Anyway, I explained to Simon why I came out to his home and asked him if he was at the powwow. Might know, he was the one who bought the quilt. Simon told me his grandson, Santana, took it with him. He had just paid for his own apartment in Lawton and started work at the Goodyear tire plant. Santana barely had anything, so he slept on a pallet of blankets. I hated to take the quilt if he didn't barely have any himself. Maybe I could offer him a replacement. I'd have to talk to him first. I called Santana four days in a row before he finally answered.

"I work the night shift," he said, and then hung up the phone.

Ah'guh! Suppose Simon could have told me that.

I called him again just after eating dinner and I apologized right away, "Your grandfather didn't say."

"Sorry, Big Sister. I didn't mean to hang up on an elder."

He was good friends with Leander and they'd grown up together in Lawton. Might know, Leander helped him get the job at Goodyear. Santana knew about Ever, but he didn't realize that Ever had sold that quilt to his grandfather.

"Can you look at the corners of the quilt for me?"

I could hear him moving around. A door opened and shut. I heard the rustling of some blankets.

"Is there a name embroidered in one of the corners?" I asked him.

It was quiet for a moment, and then I heard him say "Shiloh."

Santana told me how Leander had talked about Shiloh like he was a son. He'd wanted to spend more time with him, but Goodyear had them on twelve-hour shifts and always needed workers on overtime. Santana had met Shiloh a few times, but mostly it was Leander who told him about Shiloh's behavior, like how he busted windows on abandoned buildings, pocketed cigarettes at the Convenience Store, and stole bikes at Central Mall. Ever blamed himself, too. He'd started to work with a small group home, only "as needed," but some days he was around to spend time with Shiloh and other days he wasn't. Then Shiloh and his friends started hanging around the Rola Set. Those kids liked to send Shiloh and his friends to do things. Bad things, like beating up drunks outside bars to steal their money.

"Shiloh had this rage about him when we first met," Santana told me. "He reminded me of Leander. Well, the old Leander."

Ever worked shifts others didn't want, pushing himself in awful ways to make ends meet. Sure enough, there was one night in particular. Ever had had to work late. Too, he was exhausted, like anyone would be. He walked through his front door and found Shiloh sitting on the kitchen floor. He wouldn't look up. Right away, he sent Shandi to her room. Good thing Shawn was at a basketball game. Vomit spread around Shiloh and down his chest. Shiloh looked up

222 • Oscar Hokeah

at Ever with glassy eyes. His head rolled on his neck. Might know, he reeked of beer. Ever reached down to pick Shiloh up, but Shiloh shoved Ever back saying, "I can handle it."

Ever wiped the vomit off Shiloh's shirt and jeans, but Shiloh punched Ever in the chest and then his face. To find a nine-year-old in that condition, to find his own son like that, it must have broken Ever's heart. It would've broken mine. Just hearing about it did. Ever let Shiloh hit him, and then he pulled off the dirty shirt and jeans and led him to the shower. Shiloh fought and screamed, yelling "I don't give a shit" over and over, and punched Ever again.

Leander walked inside the trailer home and sure enough he heard all the yelling. He rushed into the bathroom. There he saw Shiloh swinging at Ever, screaming and yelling. Leander grabbed Shiloh away from Ever and held him by the shoulders.

"What the fuck is wrong with you?" he said.

Ever had to pull Leander off of Shiloh, saying "We have to let him get out his frustration." But Leander rushed for the front door, saying, "I'm going to fuck somebody up!"

Ever cut off Leander just before he stepped outside. "I need your help. Please, stay with us."

Ever wore this desperate look, near panic, like he had lost a medicine bag and Leander was the only one who could find it. So Leander stayed. They calmed Shiloh enough to get him into pajamas. By the time they helped him into his bed, the little guy was so tired that he fell asleep before the blankets were pulled over his shoulders.

After that, Leander had had enough of the View. He talked to Ever about moving to the north side—near Fort Sill—or to the newer houses built on the east side. Leander told Ever he'd help with the bills, but Ever wouldn't hear it. He told Leander, "A parent takes care of his kids, the kids don't take care of their parent."

Ever just wanted to land a full-time job at a good facility—youth-focused. Any youth. Native or not. He just wanted to be a positive influence on young people, the way his family had done for him. Hardworking people were fueled by dreams and faith. Ever imagined a four-bedroom home with a front and back yard. He dreamed of a basketball half-court, more walls for artwork, and space for toys. A part of him just knew his kids would flourish if he could just give them the things they needed to heal.

Might know, Leander asked to work a split shift at Goodyear. Good thing, too, because now he had more time with Shiloh, taking him to the movies or playing video games. Leander had so much anger at the world. Sure he still had his bad days, haw, but he learned to control himself. He was once like Shiloh—maybe worse, though, and he had so much to teach him. "You don't have to punk out," Leander told him, "Head back home when things start looking bad." All he had to do was mention Leander's name. Then those gang members wouldn't give him such a hard time. Leander showed Shiloh his drawing pad. It was filled with images of lowriders, but it was also filled with images of Lawton. Leander drew empty lots straddled by churches, the Convenience Store, broken merry-go-rounds, and random street signs. Might know, he had an eye for the grittiness of Lawton. The city's beauty, or the way he drew cracked street tops filled with black tar, like it was a treasure map to Lawton's soul—rough, rugged, and adored. Leander loved Lawton. Sure enough, Shiloh flipped through the pages, mesmerized, and Leander said, "Lawton is the city that raised me."

He gave Shiloh a stack of drawing pads and drawing pencils and told him, "When you get pissed, I want you to draw."

Shiloh had to stay in the after-school program, rather than riding the bus home. Too, Ever found a second part-time job, and it was primarily on the weekends. Now Shiloh rode around with Ever in a big white van, happy guy, transporting elderly clients to their doctor's appointments. He didn't mind, though. It gave him time to draw. Shiloh liked drawing faces, so he drew the elders. He filled the lines in the elders' faces with his own youth, as if the creases around their eyes were like swing sets and laugh lines were funnel slides. Too, the elders enjoyed having Shiloh around. He was someone they could chat up. They told him things, like how the Mud Men came out once a year, spreading mud over their bodies to stay alive, and what it was like to ride in a horse-drawn buggy. Shiloh drew and listened to his elders carefully as Ever drove them to Lawton Indian Hospital, Wal-Mart, or sometimes to Braum's for ice cream—always making it a point to buy Shiloh a scoop of his favorite: orange sherbet.

Might know, Santana had to get ready for work, and I hated to make him late.

"What color is the quilt?" I asked, trying my best to hurry.

It was orange and yellow. I told Santana about Shiloh's great-grandmother, Lena, and my quilt, and then I asked him if I could purchase the quilt.

I still had that money that Angela wouldn't take. "I can give you $1000 for it," I said, and added, "I don't want you to be without a blanket."

"Big sister," Santana said. "You can take it for free."

By the next day, Simon Kopepassah knocked on my front door. The orange and yellow made the bird patterns look like a flock of robins. And there it was in a corner of the quilt—Shiloh's embroidered name.

IT WAS MAYBE same day, or next day after, but I spoke with my cousin Lila, again. This time for Shandi; her quilt was the last. And might know, Lila surprised me with news.

"I'm sorry I didn't get you one of those quilts, Opbee." Ever had told her, when he stopped by Lila's house to pick up Shandi after work. "I gave Shandi's quilt to Jimena," he had said.

Bay'gaw!

I couldn't believe my big ol' Kiowa ears. Why did he give

it to that ma'bane? Now I didn't want to show up out of nowhere on Jimena's doorstep, but haw'nay I had no choice. There was a frustration growing inside of me. I thought about my own mother, how she'd left me and my sisters all those years ago, didn't even love us enough to return. I was so sick of all these fractured families. Tired of it. Children being left in so much pain. It was wrong. I remembered how I'd changed my pain into anger to survive. How could someone who abandoned her children also rob them of their only way to heal? Why would Jimena even take the quilt when it was offered to her? And why in the hell would my nah'ee give it to her in the first place? I had to fix this mess, if not for Shandi, then for Lena, and certainly for the good of naw thep'thay'gaw—our family. It was like a trigger, knowing Jimena took Shandi's quilt. Might know, I found myself standing on Jimena's doorstep, trying to convince myself to knock. But before I had the chance, she opened the door.

"Can I help you?"

I had a really good speech, too. Jimena already knew about Lena and the quilts, but she didn't know about *my* quilt. I would explain to her straight and clear: Lena healed me. She had the wisdom to heal multiple generations in her family, including Shandi, and then I'd land on details in the quilts, like the symbols of the colors and patterns. It was a beautifully thought-out speech, but that's not what I said.

"How could you, after everything, take a quilt from a little?"

Jimena's face immediately went pale.

I suppose mine, too, and I heard the anger in my own words, real bitter, regretting as soon as they left my mouth.

Then Jimena did something that took me by surprise: she invited me in.

Jimena was ya'koi day'he'thay—a beautiful young lady. Her spirit was much like my daughter's, where she was so smart and quick-minded, yet her gentleness kept her from being intimidating. Sure enough, I took to her like a shawl over shoulders. She asked me questions about the family and I confided. And I would never have asked about her past, or how her and my nah'ee broke up, and I didn't, but she told me. I must've wrapped her in my own shawl, because she divulged more than I expected.

Like with her child, Baby Turtle, telling me about how she passed away. Zadle'bay! She needed to tell someone, it was so sad, so terrible, and maybe she needed to tell it to a mother. I was willing to be that person for her, Jimena, and she said it was a deep depression that destroyed her marriage with Ever. It came to her in dreams—the sadness. And the more I thought about depression, the more I realized it had always hit me the hardest at night. Maybe that was why I needed Lena's quilt when I was a young mau'tawn. And maybe it was from the pain of losing my mother. Jimena said she'd wake from her sleep and sit on the edge of the bed for hours, Ever asleep beside her, and she sat there in the dark—not saying a single word. Too, her mind raced with memories of her baby. Could she have done more? Should she have done more? Her baby would be five years old now, starting kindergarten, calling her momma. She sat there in the dark, Jimena, thinking about what it would feel like to hold a five-year-old little girl in her lap.

Worse still, Ever would find her sitting on the stairs or sitting in her car—her expression always vacant. He took her on trips to Tahlequah to get her out of Lawton, and convinced her to sign up for classes at Cameron University. She went to conferences for Hispanic culture and community development. She tried to be interested in things, but most days she couldn't find a reason. Haw, there was always someone better, smarter, stronger than her. Or so her sadness told her anyway. But something had to give. Either she had to end the marriage, or the depression would end everything.

Once it was over, she didn't expect to see Shawn, Shiloh, and Shandi, anymore. Maybe at Wal-Mart, or a park, too, if she was driving by. Then there was a knock on her front door. Jimena answered. Ah'guh, no one was outside. A text popped up on her phone: "I left you a gift." Ever had placed Shandi's quilt on her porch, as an invite of sorts. Sometimes marriages ended like a powwow trick song, making dancers stumble instead of stop. Might know, Shandi was stumbling. Then Jimena saw the quilt's violet and mauve atop bird patterns—she remembered, and her tension eased.

After they started talking, Ever told her how he'd found

bite marks on Shandi's arm. Ever described Shandi's anger as a quiet violence. She was a true dolly, but also somehow more aggressive than the boys. She didn't just play with her toys, haw'nay, she always took them apart, breaking them. Ever showed Jimena Shandi's Barbie dolls that she had burned on the stove, the fingers cut off of their plastic hands. Her teddy bears with their insides pulled out. Shandi found ways to destroy almost every toy.

After my nah'ee found the first bite marks on the back of her hand, he asked her who had showed her how to do that. She said a kid in her class. Then one day Shandi had three large bite marks on her left forearm. They weren't indentions. They were bruises, circular in the shape of her teeth. Sure enough, I remembered when I was a young mau'tawn, how I'd sunk my teeth into my own skin.

Worse still, when Ever asked Shandi to do small things, little things like clean her room, she'd fly into a temper tantrum. He'd ask her to pick up her toys or make her bed, right before something she enjoyed. Or if they were going to Braum's for ice cream, he told the kids to clean their rooms. But Shandi would walk to her room and shut the door, refusing to clean up anything. She rejected every treat to the point that she no longer had sweets.

Ever had had enough. He was tired. He was working all the time. He told her that if she didn't clean her room, he would throw all of her toys in the trash. Shandi ran to her room, slammed the door shut, and screamed. Ever rushed down the hallway. Shandi had scratched herself across her cheeks and down her neck, leaving red lines. Then she pulled her hair as hard as she could, crying the whole time. Ever grabbed her hands and pulled them away, told her haw'nay, no, stop, but she kept at it. When she couldn't get to her hair, she slipped her hand into her mouth, clamping onto the skin between her thumb and pointer finger. Ever dropped to one knee—eye level—and tried to shove his own fingers into Shandi's mouth. He kept yelling, "Stop, Shandi, stop!" It only made her bite harder. Her face turned red. Through clamped teeth and skin, she screamed and screamed.

Ever pried his fingers into Shandi's mouth. He managed to get her teeth apart, pulled her arms to her side, and pinned her down. My nah'ee had been trained in group homes to place youth in holds. Never did he think his own daughter. Might know, there he was grabbing Shandi's arms, pinning them against her sides, and holding her to the floor. Screaming, she kicked her heels into his knees. She threw her head backward and caught him in the mouth. Ever flinched at the headbutt. He held her and let her scream. He let her cry. He let her kick him. He held her until she was too tired to kick anymore, until she was too tired to cry, until her muscles released their tension and she went limp in his arms. So he let her go. Shandi lay on her bedroom floor, sobbing. Ever lay down next to her and ran a hand over her hair, shushing into her ear like when she was a baby.

"Ever asked if I could help," Jimena said, and then she

smiled because she was happy to reconnect with the kids. There was something about her smile, too, sweet and soft. I always thought those smiles were the best—the ones connected to children. It not only told me the darkest of her depression was fading, but it seemed to put me at ease. I wanted to share my story. The one about Lena's quilt. But I suppose, more important, how it connected to my own mother. By the end of our visit, not only were we both crying, we were holding each other, like I became the daughter she needed and she became the mother I never had.

She handed me Shandi's quilt. "Could you take this back to her? Opbee, I'd like you to be the one."

THAT VERY NEXT weekend the Oklahoma Gourd Dance Club hosted a benefit powwow for the Taptto family. "We'll be at the Comanche Complex," Lila told me, and my best bet was to catch Ever there. Quinton had asked Ever to be Head Man, and those two were near enough twins—like Sun Boy split in half.

I spotted Shawn, Shiloh, and Shandi before I saw Ever. The boys were a pair of dreamboats. They wore matching red vests under bandoliers made with mescal beads. Their red-and-navy-blue sash belts showed red in the front, Gkoi way, and the beadwork matched the red-and-blue pattern on their gourds. Shandi wore the brightest red shawl I had ever seen. Navy-blue fringe hung from the shawl's base and sides. She wore a traditional cloth dress in a matching red, with seashells across the chest and shoulders. She had beautiful white and red hair barrettes to hold back two pigtails.

Ever stood nearby in a black dress shirt and khaki dress pants. Too, his red-and-navy-blue sash was draped around his neck—real ki'ee. As I walked up to him, I saw military patches on the left side—red side—of his sash. Haw! He held a rattle in one hand, a tin salt and pepper shaker. He carried an eagle feather fan in the other. I called out to him, "You're so handsome."

Sure enough, he turned, and his eyes went straight to the stack of quilts in my arms. All four folded and nearly covering my face. Leander quickly stepped next to Ever. His eyes trained on the quilts. From all I'd heard about him, I had always imagined Leander to look much meaner, like Chief White Horse in those old photos. But he wore slacks and a button-down white shirt with a red tie. More like tribal council than a former gang member. His long, black hair was in the same tight ponytail as Ever's, and might know, he wore a similar red-and-navy-blue sash.

"Is that my blanket?" Leander asked before I had a chance to speak.

Next thing, Shawn, Shiloh, and Shandi noticed, rushed over. Suddenly, I had the entire family staring at the quilts in my arms. Buh, I felt like a bowl of bote with all those hungry eyes staring at me.

"Your great-grandma made magic quilts," I said. I pulled off each and handed them to their rightful owners. I even caught big, bad Leander smiling. Shawn almost yanked his quilt out of my arms, and Shiloh had the biggest eyes.

I sat in a nearby chair and pulled Shandi to my side. Carefully, I gave her the quilt, and said, "Your great-grandma gave me a quilt like this a very long time ago."

She hugged her quilt, and then reached out to hug me. Her smile flashed a set of bright teeth. It was the kind of smile that easily melted an old lady.

"Big Sister told me all about her magic quilts," Shandi said. "They chase away monsters in the night."

I held Shandi an extra moment and sent a silent prayer to Lena. The love she had for her family was laced within every piece of thread stitched across her quilts. It was Lena who held us all together.

Ever Geimausaddle
(2013)

BEHIND THE COUNTER at the Cherokee Nation Housing Authority stood a skaw-stee guy, staring. The only words this evil sop'ho managed to say: "We're taking the first fifty applications." It was an off chance, but my only chance. So I prayed.

IT WAS ABOUT five o'clock—evening—when I drove through the parking lot of the Gregg Glass Community Building. Two people already sat in lawn chairs outside the glass doors. I thought, "Desperate, guys." Tla, la vidad, I was about to do the same. The front doors to the community building wouldn't open until eight o'clock in the morning. My coworkers had told me to get there right away, that a line formed the day before. Gaa, I didn't believe them. Not until I saw.

Guess the fire was built. I had no choice. I drove my car through the roundabout and headed back to my sister's house, hurrying. When I walked through the front door, I shouted to Sissy to lend me her phone charger. My iPhone was fully charged, but phones die faster than the sun sets and it'd be dark soon enough. I loaded up a powwow chair, a fleece throw, a pillow, snacks, and a bottle of Sprite. My mom stepped out of her room with an old quilt in her arms.

"It'll keep you warm through the night," she said.

Despite it looking thin and old, the quilt was in good condition. "I've been saving it for you, Ever," she told me. It was one of my grandma Lena's quilts, with Bird Clan symbols. Saving it for me? Why had I not seen it before? I had to run so I didn't have time to ask. Sissy handed me her charger.

"Call me if you need anything," she said.

Before though, I had to drop Leander at work, over at Subway.

"My boss from Goodyear wrote on my Facebook wall," Leander told me. "She's wanting me to come back to Lawton." When we'd moved to Tahlequah, Leander left a good job so he could stay close to the family. And he didn't have to; there was plenty of family to take him in. Aunt Lila and Uncle Hank were the first to offer. I was proud of him for choosing to move with us though. I had been spinning my wheels for years and so tired of juggling two part-time jobs. Barely having enough to pay rent. My sister kept telling me, "There are good jobs in Tahlequah," so eventually I gave in. She'd opened her home to me and my kids, but Leander wasn't adjusting well to the lack of space. Might know, he made comments about moving back to Lawton within the first week of living in Tahlequah. Good thing he landed the job at Subway or he would have already left.

"You'll have your own room when I get one of these homes," I told him just before he climbed out of the car.

Leander looked me in the eyes, slid his Subway visor onto his head, and stared at me like I was ma'bane. He was uha-hnalun about work so he didn't say another word. He opened the door, climbed out, and walked to the front doors of Subway. I hated that he was so frustrated.

I wound my way back to Swimmer housing addition—I'd been gone maybe thirty minutes, forty minutes tops, but there were already two more people standing in line. As I climbed out of my car, two other vehicles drove by slowly— just like I had before. I hurried myself to the line, unfolded my lawn chair, and took my place in the fifth spot.

A blond lady with an OU shirt smiled at me and shifted her chair to give me a little more room. She introduced herself as Davetta, and asked, "Are you from Tahlequah?"

"Yes and no," I told her, as I turned my chair to face her more directly.

I started to give Davetta my routine answer since moving back to Tahlequah from Lawton, but in the end told her the whole story. I lived with my sister, who'd inherited the house from our mother, Turtle, who received the home through the Housing Authority years ago. Cherokee Nation would not be building any more new homes, the new Principal Chief made that clear. The only way you could get one now was through the distribution of repossessed houses. My sister had her two kids and also cared for our aging mother. I had my four kids, so when we moved in, a full house became a dormitory. My sister slept with her kids in the master bedroom, my mother had her own room, and I shared a room with Shawn, Shiloh, and Shandi. Leander slept on the living room couch.

When I heard Cherokee Nation had fifty repossessed homes to give to Cherokee citizens, I couldn't miss the date. Saved it for months on my calendar. Here was a chance to get a forever home. Specifically for my kids, or I would lose them. Shawn and Shiloh had been saying how they could move in with Leander, or live with their Grandma Lila. Then Shandi started to mention how she missed fishing with her stepmother, Jimena. Now she had weekly phone calls with Jimena, but they weren't the same as biweekly visits.

Fortunately, I saw a little hope after they met their

biological mother for the first time. I say for the first time because they'd been just oos-di, one, two, and three years old, when I left Tahlequah for Lawton all those years ago. Now they were eleven, twelve, and thirteen, and their mother heard I was back in Tahlequah so she found me on Facebook. Why did I let the reunion happen? Maybe I still felt guilty for what I had done all those years ago, maybe I was back in town to atone for what I had done, but maybe I thought it would give the kids a reason to stay. I had mixed the excitement of moving to Tahlequah with the potential for visiting their ae-jee. They didn't act excited, or repulsed, by the idea; they were more indifferent.

I hadn't seen Lonnie Nowater in over ten years. I had no idea she would show up to McDonald's in stained jeans and a jacket, where the zipper on one side had come completely off. But it wasn't just the way she dressed. She smiled at the kids and I saw how half her teeth were rotted out. She told me that she'd been clean for over five years, but she was oosa-tle and fidgeted with the straw in her drink. She glanced between the boys fighting over their fries and Shandi drinking her milkshake too fast. It looked like she was nervous, but then she said, "I'm living over on the other side . . . take the bypass . . . do you think the kids . . ." and then dropped completely silent when she started fidgeting with her straw again. She didn't have any scabs or track marks, but I couldn't help but wonder if she was tweaking. Only a baboso would show up high to visit their kids. Then she said something that made me pause. "I'm learning to love, Ever." It was the only clear sentence she said the entire visit. A trickle of hope rose inside of me like water. Our babies deserved a chance to know their mother. I couldn't deny the truth.

As we drove away from the visit, Shandi asked, "Can a kid have more than one mom?"

"Your Grandma Turtle and Grandma Lila are both my mothers," I told her, and it made me a little proud to reinforce traditional kinship customs with my daughter.

"Because they're sisters," she said, and asked, "Can I call Jimena when we get home?"

Then Shawn said, "I was a little scared at first," and Shiloh echoed, "Me, too."

As we drove down Muskogee Avenue, all three asked me, "Will she always be like that?" like triplets reading each other's minds.

"I don't know, babe," I told them, "But we'll have to visit her again to find out."

Was it my guilty conscience? The way I left Lonnie all those years ago, tormenting her until she loved the misery of meth more than the misery of my revenge. With one of these homes, the kids would grow up here in Tahlequah, and maybe Lonnie and I could redeem ourselves with the hearts of our children. I certainly couldn't go back to living in a rundown trailer in the worst part of Lawton. Tahlequah was a small town with problems that didn't seem like problems, not compared to the problems on the south-side of Lawton, in the View. Sure there were isolated families like the Nowaters, but Tahlequah was so small-town I could leave my car unlocked. In fact, on the first night I did exactly that. Accidentally, of course. I was exhausted from moving boxes. Worse still, I left my phone in the car. The next morning I woke in a panic and rushed outside. But I found my phone sitting on the passenger seat and the change in the console.

My sister told me, "It was divine intervention." As soon as I arrived in Tahlequah, I applied for youth-focused work, what I'd always done, and within two weeks, I was offered a job at the John A. Ketcher Youth Shelter. Full-time work at Cherokee Nation with good pay and options for insurance. It happened so quickly, and it was difficult to not wonder if it really was divine intervention. My kids were the center of my world, but it would be hard for me to walk away from this new job. It was a small miracle to have something positive to work toward. I had spent so much of my career helping disadvantaged Native youth, doing anything else would've felt meaningless.

In bed at night, my mind raced with the worst possible scenario.

Leander would leave first.

Shiloh would want to follow because Leander was like a second father to him.

Then Shawn would follow Shiloh.

Shandi would ask to move in with Jimena, I was certain.

It would take convincing Leander. Once he stayed, the other three would stay. But if I couldn't give him a good reason, then he would put me in a tough position. One that might split naw thep'thay'gaw apart.

So there I was, sitting in a lawn chair, prepared to sit in the same spot through the entire night just for the off chance I might win one of Cherokee Nation's fifty repossessed homes.

"I'm sorry," I said to Davetta, "for having just dumped my life into your lap. All this just happened so fast I can't really believe it."

"Dump away," she said, laughed, and then asked, "Who's your family?"

"I'm a Stopp," I told her, "But my last name is Geimausaddle. I'm Kiowa and Cherokee."

"Oh, wow, I married a Stopp," she said. She threw her head back and laughed. Then added, "I divorced him. You Stopp boys can't seem to keep your pants up when a pretty girl winks at you."

I smiled and laughed awkwardly.

"I'm just playing with you," she said and pushed my shoulder. "I'm teasing."

I knew, and she knew, she wasn't teasing. But we chuckled as if we didn't know. It led to more talk. Good thing, too, because it was going to be a long night.

Come to find out, the guy she divorced was one of my

Cherokee primos—my mother's uncle Bradley had ten sons and one daughter. Those pre-Nintendo numbers. Davetta was around my age—mid thirties—and was very talkative. She pulled out her smartphone—the newest Samsung—and swiped through pictures of her son. He was ten years old and an avid baseball player. He had clear Stopp family features. Characteristics I didn't have, eyes a little more narrow and sharp cheekbones, like my grandmother and her brother. I took more after my mother, who took more after her Kiowa father, but more so her Kiowa great-grandmother than him. I looked at the pictures on Davetta's phone and could see reflections of my family looking back. Funny how relations grew as we got older—more years, more kin.

When Davetta and I stopped talking, we were surprised to find about ten more newcomers on the sidewalk, lined up for the off chance to win a forever home. She said, "Is this a hog fry before the Stomp Dance?" and laughed at herself. I laughed, too, although I hadn't been to a Stomp since I was a teenager. Cherokees lined the sidewalk like a bucket of hog meat stood at the front door.

A few newcomers took their place in line as more trickled in from the duplexes that surrounded the community building. Within a few hours, the line grew to eighteen people. Someone in the crowd bellowed a loud turkey call just as the sun disappeared over the horizon. Powwow chairs in almost every color stretched from the front door down the sidewalk. People continued to drift in as darkness climbed over the duplexes. By ten thirty, the line grew to twenty-five people, and all the voices between family, friends, and spouses carried into the night and filled the air from Ross Swimmer over toward Muskogee Avenue.

At the first sign of heavy clouds, someone said, "Weather's supposed to get a little rough tonight." We kept our eyes trained on the sky, waiting.

The storm hit the trees first. Under gusts of wind, leaves clamored and branches tossed. Next we felt trickles of water on our cheeks and shoulders. Then distant lightning flashed behind heavy clouds and gave us a quick moment to see what was heading in our direction. Then the sky fell into a deeper darkness, like our eyes closed and our bodies became moving shapes behind our eyelids. Soon the sprinkles turned into heavy drops of cold water. We flinched as the rain landed on our backs and heads, cringing. A voice in the group called out, "Let's make a zigzag pattern under the porch." We all lined up and down the narrow porch, trying our best to stay out of the rain. Barely past eleven o'clock, and everyone was already on top of each other. It was going to be a long night. As uncomfortable as we were, with just inches of space between bodies, it was better than cold rain on our backs.

The drops quickly turned into a heavy downpour. I huddled closer to Davetta as she extended a blanket toward me, and I pulled out the quilt Mom had given me. I looked over the bird patterns and thought about my grandmother, Lena, remembering. When did she make this quilt? It looked old. Then I noticed my name embroidered in one of the corners of the quilt: Ever. It was mine? There was so much I needed to ask my mother, but I was distracted by the cold rain falling just outside the porch.

Davetta and I sat next to the wall, but the splash of raindrops sent a cold mist onto our exposed faces. This was a night when we envied turtles, as we huddled underneath the porch as if it were a shell.

The lightning came in as heavy and as fast as the rain. The first shot of thunder rolled from a few miles away. People in the crowd counted down. Then the thunder slammed in unison with the lightning above us. We flinched, and then cringed. Each flash blinded us, and each clap of thunder made us move a little closer together.

A loud *crack!* whipped the air, and behind the flash there was an explosion. Sparks shot out from a transformer on a pole near Muskogee Avenue. We yelled out in surprise, and a vibration moved through us, as though a current of electricity tied us all together. It was our fear. We came to our feet and peered past the trees and buildings, trying to see if the transformer had fallen. Then all the lights in the neighborhood turned off. A deeper darkness covered us and we all went silent, listening. We only heard rain and wind cutting through the trees. Somewhere in the distance sirens and horns blared in response to the shattered transformer.

The storm was uha-hnalun, and we all knew it wouldn't

stop soon. A tall lady from the Hogshooter family yelled, "I called someone and they're bringing us tarps." She stood next to her brother, who was the same height. We said back, "wa-do," and "oosd" and "ho-wa-ju," and then we sat back down into our chairs, huddling inside blankets and against each other. The mother to the Hogshooter siblings drove into the parking lot less than ten minutes later on break from Hastings Hospital and delivered us six tarps. She had the same strong jawline and towering height as her kids. We all came to our feet. The son went to his truck and came back with a thick roll of duct tape. Together we unrolled the tarps under the rain and against the wind—the lightning and thunder had moved on to a different part of Oklahoma. We spread the tarp wide and long between the posts. We used the duct tape to fasten one side to the pole and we used screwdrivers to root the tarp into the ground. While most of them were big enough to spread from ground to ceiling, one tarp was too small. The brother Hogshooter stood from his powwow chair like a giant rising from the forest, with rain still gushing in, and held the tarp to the top of the porch. His sister quickly grabbed the opposite end. We grabbed the other corners. We had prayed under our breaths to shape-shift us all into a single, unified turtle and couldn't help but smile at what we had become. We stayed fixed in that position for what felt like hours, with the muscles in our arms and legs hurting with exhaustion. The heavy rains became lighter and the winds let the rain fall straight down. Soon

or the cold?" We laughed between bites, and soon we chatted about how and why we were so desperate to have one of the fifty repossessed homes.

The Hogshooter sister had a toddler boy and was now expecting an oos-di—four months along. The brother would be off to college soon but the Hogshooter household would get tighter over the next few years. "My mother has already done a lot for us," the sister said. She and her husband were ready to have a home of their own and a place where their kids could grow. The brother said how he might be sleeping on the couch once his sister had her baby. He told us, "It'd only be on the school breaks," but there was a crack in his voice.

It was the Nofires who told us how their trailer's floors had rotted out, and their landlord wouldn't fix anything. They lived at the trailer park by the Elks Lodge, south of town. Everyone in Tahlequah knew about the landlord making methamphetamine in vacant trailers. "We have three kids," the Nofires said, and they were playing around meth chemicals. There was always an odor like someone had just fumigated because of the cooking going on in different trailers. It would've been nice if the landlord would fumigate to get rid of the cockroaches. The Nofires refused to pay rent one month to get him to spray for bugs, and he filed small claims against them. The Nofires said, "We need to have our kids somewhere decent to live."

The Fishinghawks lived three families to their mother's

old Cherokee Nation home. She had inherited it from her mother. It was one of the first Indian homes built in the Tahlequah area, out past Stick Ross Mountain Road—just north of Sequoyah High School. Their mother was wheelchair bound. They also had two siblings and one cousin. Everybody had kids. One of the siblings was married. In total, there were seven children between them. They'd made a three-bedroom house into a four-bedroom house by converting the living room to a bedroom, with each family trying to have their own space. Their mother navigated an obstacle course getting her wheelchair to the kitchen or bathroom. She shared a room with two of her grandchildren.

The Marble family wanted to move out of Stilwell, to get away from meth. Their nephew, who worked at McDonald's, was offered a pipe right at the drive-thru window. It was a car full of girls. When he turned them down, one of them barked, "What? You don't want to lose your minimum-wage job?" They drove off laughing. One police officer sold meth because he was addicted himself. "It's bad when the state police have to arrest local police," the Marble family said. The officer had gone to jail, but the police from the top down were as corrupt as the gang members. "No one in Stilwell wants to clean it up," one of Marbles said. "They're either profiting from it or addicted to it or both." The families who stayed away from meth were robbed by random people and sometimes even their own relatives. No one could go to the Wal-Mart without running the risk of getting killed over eighty dollars.

The Hogshooters brought up the Copeland family and how their relative was the director of the Cherokee Nation Housing Authority. Ma'bane had funneled a home for every relative down to her nieces and nephews. "She should go to prison," the Hogshooter sister said, and the brother followed with "All those homes should be repossessed for Cherokees who didn't cheat." It would mean fifty more homes for the community. All Cherokees had a fair chance to get a home, supposedly. On the day when repossessed homes were offered to community members, everyone was to receive identical paperwork. Every family completed the paperwork at the same time, on the same day, and had equal chance to hand it in. But the Copeland family got everything early, and it was all completed before they stepped through the doors. The Copelands would stroll up to the counter, hand over the forms, and secure their homes. Every other Cherokee scrambled to complete the directives and fill in each line—before all the homes were taken. And so every adult in the Copeland family had ended up with a home each, while most Cherokee families were crammed into one.

The Nofires said the Thompson family already had a home in the husband's name and then the wife lined up on the last home distribution to secure a second one. "How can someone cheat their own community?" one of the

Nofires asked. Come to find out, the husband worked for the Housing Authority and cheated on his wife with the director. The wife had kids from a previous marriage and this was her way of securing a home for herself; soon after she had all the paperwork finalized, she filed for divorce. "Must have been some type of payoff," one of the Nofires said. The Thompson husband continued to live in the first home—a three-bedroom—by himself. People in the community spread gawo-nisgi about the director's car parked in his driveway every Thursday around lunchtime.

The Fishinghawks told how a mon'sape program manager at the Housing Authority took money under the table from Nacirema Risk Management Corporation, and then told the new Cherokee homeowners this company was the only option for homeowner's insurance. "People were just happy to get a house," the Fishinghawks said. It was mandatory for them to insure the home while paying off their debt to the Housing Authority, and Nacirema doubled the prices for Cherokee citizens. Local insurance companies could have easily offered them lower rates—if they knew. "We'll repossess your home," the program manager told the new homeowners as they signed their paperwork. She always went on about her vacations to Hawaii and leased a new Lexus every single year.

The Marbles said the applications manager at the Housing Authority was "like a brown toad." He was skaw-stee and weeded through applications to get rid of anyone from

Muskogee. "They might be associated with the Freedmen," he had slipped once and said out loud. People in the Housing Authority office talked about him turning away Cherokees who were part Black. According to him, there were never any homes available. Not until they were built or repossessed. Most people didn't know the process. But he wasn't about to explain anything. If people didn't know the questions to ask, then why give them reasons to inquire? This sop'ho guy published policy that read like a "Not Open for Business" sign. People who applied for new construction or repossessed homes worked in factories or frontline retail. Most didn't know to ask. Even when Freedmen did ask for an application, it was pointless to fill out because the pinche cabrone would run it through a shredder.

As the stories dwindled, light from our smartphones lit up the darkness under the porch like fireflies huddled for safety. We checked our Facebook profiles and we checked the time. One person yawned so the rest of us yawned. There was a cascade through the group like an echo. Our eyelids dropped like tarps. We pulled blankets over our shoulders. We shimmied a little closer to the people beside us. Those of us who had pillows laid them on the backs of our chairs. Those of us who didn't have pillows rested our heads against other heads or atop shoulders. The chatter became less and less as voices lowered. The night was cold but the rains had stopped. The wind continued to rustle the trees, swaying leaves and branches like a lullaby, singing.

Before any of our phones hit 2 a.m., we were all asleep, and likely dreaming of our first-time forever home.

WHEN I OPENED my eyes, the line had doubled. The sun rose over a cloudless, blue sky. The newcomers in front of Gregg Glass Community Building had lined up by the parking lot and down the street. I woke confused by the haziness of the day and by the sleep in my eyes. I climbed out of my lawn chair and folded my quilt under the first rays of a rising sun. I carried both to the trunk of my car and returned to take my spot at number five in line. The others unformed the zigzag line under the porch, made a straight line to the sidewalk, and connected to the newcomers. I picked up the trash laying around my area and threw it into a large black bag. One of the others carried it off to a dumpster. Sleep lingered in my eyes like the memory of gawo-nisgi shared between families.

The small parking lot filled quickly and cars had to park alongside the street. More and more people made their way over to the sidewalk. Soon the newcomers were stretched further down the street and nearing the corner where McSpadden met Hensley Street. They filled the sidewalk from Gregg Glass Community Building down to the Housing Authority's Management Building. Between 7:00 a.m. and 7:30, the line grew from fifty to one hundred people. Ten minutes before the doors were to open, the line had grown past two hundred people. Voices cascaded as if flocks of birds filled the surrounding trees. Pockets of conversation fluctuated with waves of banter and gossip.

The front doors opened. The line vanished.

I felt an unsettling rush as I stepped inside the building and felt the crowd behind me surge into the large room. I was handed a clipboard, pen, and a stack of papers. Tired from the night in a lawn chair, I stumbled over to the long tables in the center of the room. The newcomers, just out of their cars, had energy to complete the forms quickly. More and more bodies filled the community building. There were nearly two hundred people inside a building only capable of holding half as much. Those with only one child completed the forms within a minute. Those with the most children took the longest. I thought of Leander moving back to Lawton, Shiloh following him, and then Shawn. How could I raise Shandi away from her brothers? I wrote fast—near scribbles—but legible enough to discern all the names that filled in the boxes. I was groggy and my hand cramped, but I pushed myself to write faster.

I was caught between bodies when I stood from the table and made a dash for the front. Three attendants stood behind one long counter. The attendants took the forms, flipped through each page to examine if they had been completed properly. Then each application was stamped with a number under the weight of a heaving, mechanized click.

I pushed and shoved and jostled against the crowd as a wave attempted to move forward. I squeezed between shoulders. I shimmied around bodies. I felt the space between people filling with desperation. I heard a Hogshooter bark, "What number were you?" I was hit with elbows and heard a Marble apologize with, "I didn't see you there." A Nofire mumbled nervously when I heard a Fishinghawk announce, "They're at number forty." Then the wave swayed forward and bodies began to crush between the weight of people behind and in front.

The attendants took applications and said nothing, their faces tight and nervous, like the people in the crowd. They stamped each application and I counted down. Grab and stamp, grab and stamp, grab and stamp. 41 to 42 to 43 to 44. Grab and stamp. They didn't dare look at the crowd. They stared at forms, at stamps, and at their hands. Grab and stamp. 45 to 46 to 47. The attendants glanced at each other when one said, "I have number forty-eight." I ducked under the large arms of a Hogshooter as I rushed forward. Two hundred bodies in this small room, tla, made even smaller by desperation. The attendants took a half step backward. I knocked a Marble to my right and cutoff a Fishinghawk to my left. The attendants glanced at each other and said, "Keep stamping," and I saw the desperate crowd reflected in their eyes. I never heard the call of forty-nine. I slammed my application down onto the counter, and with the unsettling click of a mechanized stamp, I was named #50.

NOWADAYS, I STEP onto my new wooden deck in the mornings to greet the sun—grateful. I pull my medicine bag from my pocket, untie the leather strap, and then dip my fingers into the tobacco. I lift my hand out of the medicine bag and bring the tobacco up to my mouth. I breathe my spirit into it, like medicine. Then I extend my hand toward the rising sun and sprinkle the tobacco, offering. I pray for everyone across Earth. I pray for the Hogshooters, the Marbles, and the Fishinghawks, I tell the sun, "Daw'kee aim'boh," knowing all that I have done. I think of Lonnie, and I add, "Ah kaw'awn," for our children, hoping, praying they will understand, each will understand, how our forever home kept us intact. I call "Day'on'day" to the sun, and then I ask, tla, I beg, I say, "Forgive me."

Acknowledgments

I'D LIKE TO pay respect to my hometowns, Tahlequah and Lawton, Oklahoma—to the streets and landscapes that shaped the edges of my personality.

My mother, Virgilene Chavez (Hokeah), for being the quiet force at my back. My babies, Jasper, Joseph, Jaxson, Baby Virgilene, Sadie, Gabby, and Hadley. I write every word for you. I'd like to thank my sisters, Regina Phillips and Ignacia "Tweet" Chavez, for setting me straight when I was wrong and picking me up when I was down. I'll always be grateful. For the Tahsequah side of my family, Linda, Butch, Quincy, Terry, Mabel, and Joetta, for always protecting and guiding me—even when I least deserved it. My uncle, Vernon Hokeah, for being a strong male role model. For the Phillips side of my family, Linda, Perry Sr., Brandon, Chris, and Perry Jr., for taking me in and making me an honorary member of their tribe.

I want to give a special wa-do to Toby and Valorie Hughes. Thank you for helping me with many of the Cherokee words in this novel. More, thank you for being patient with a chubby little Indian boy always showing up at your store, so many years ago. I'll remember Chero-Hawk fondly, as will many of us in Tahlequah. Thank you, Toby, for gifting me the flute. I'll think of you every time I play it. And mostly, thank you for the medicine you've given me over the years. It healed more than just my body—it healed my spirit as well.

I wouldn't be here if it weren't for a host of educators. Much respect to the Institute of American Indian Arts and the English Department at the University of Oklahoma. I can't say enough about how important it is to have mentors willing to help students find more reasons to love their craft. It's a special skill and should be honored. Wa-do to the instructors who helped me along the way.

CALLING FOR
A BLANKET
DANCE

Naw Thep'thay'gaw
An Essay by Oscar Hokeah

Questions for Discussion

Naw Thep'thay'gaw

An Essay by Oscar Hokeah

MY FATHER IMMIGRATED to Oklahoma from Aldama in the state of Chihuahua, Mexico, when he was only fourteen years old, following his older cousins to work the peanut and cotton fields on the Southern Plains. My mother is a full-blood Native American, half Kiowa and half Cherokee, and she raised me between her two tribes as a single mother. Growing up in this intertribal and multicultural atmosphere, I went from traditional dances with Kiowas and Comanches to traditional dances with Cherokees and Creeks. I have vivid memories of living in old farmhouses with groups of migrant Mexican laborers, who spent their days working the red earth of the Southern Plains under the grueling heat of an Oklahoma sun. As I grew into adulthood I came to terms with the various identities informing who I am.

And it wasn't just my cultural identity, but also my shifting identity as a man. More important, how the Indigenous matriarchs around me informed who I was as a male in my tribal communities. The heart of my novel is about all of this: about family, naw thep'thay'gaw, and how families show up for each other, and about masculinity. The title comes from an important ritual in powwow culture: When we call for a blanket dance, we're asking for the community to step up and help out someone in need. The main character, Ever Geimausaddle, has a host of family members willing to do just that—willing to hear the call, step up to the edges of the blanket, and offer a piece of themselves for his greater healing. As this happens, Ever's identity becomes shaped by the family members willing to do the work.

Like Ever, I came to understand the multifarious nature of my own identity through my family. Also like Ever, I'm Kiowa, Cherokee, and Mexican. Ever is faced with a multitude of obstacles, none greater than overcoming the unattainable ideals of toxic masculinity. I knew firsthand the back-and-forth sway between traditional Indigenous values and an out-of-control patriarchy. I sought to capture the meeting spaces where tribal matriarchy clashed with hypermasculinity—especially in struggling over family and property. In this, Ever became the battleground. I knew as I wrote the novel that Ever would come to a point where the battle cries from his ancestors would break him into a million pieces, giving him no choice but to build himself back up. The larger question had to do with the possibility of his transformation. As his grandmother, Lena Stopp, asks, "Would my grandson ever be cured?"

In addition to exploring the subtle and obvious ways male-on-male violence creates toxic masculinity, I also wanted to disrupt the homogenous perception of Native Americans. Because I grew up between Kiowa and Cherokee tribes, I lived the beautiful differences of each. Oklahoma is host to thirty-nine different tribes. Each has its own language, practices, customs, and rituals. There are shared practices that bind us together, and we also share the scars of a brutal colonial history. This history unites all tribes throughout the Americas. What I felt was missing from contemporary literature was acknowledgment of the differences among us. Sometimes this manifests in intertribal conflicts, but more often than not this is the medicine that creates multicultural tribalism, where we exchange and share and gift one another practices and ideologies, such as gourd dance rituals between Kiowa and Comanche and matrilineal customs between Cherokee and Creek. The outcome is a richness in tribal cultures. In juxtaposing Kiowa and Cherokee communities, I wanted to show a dynamic of the Native American world very few consider and give readers a slice of America very few know about.

Juxtaposing two tribes was easier said than done, although initially it was easy to distinguish the differences. I knew the difference in languages, rituals, and landscapes: Kiowas were on the Southern Plains; Cherokees were in the Ozark Hills. Kiowas practiced the Gourd Dance; Cherokees, the Stomp Dance. But if that were the extent of it, then this novel would've been completed back in 2008 when I wrote one of its earliest chapters. The element that was most difficult to capture was voice. At an early stage in our development as writers we struggle with voice; it's super elusive. We can name it and see it in our favorite authors, but ask us to develop it and we find ourselves in a depth of mental torment for sometimes years, if not decades. I knew I needed to distinguish the difference between Kiowa community members and Cherokee. How was I going to accomplish this task when I couldn't even hear my own accent?

Attending the BFA Program in Creative Writing at the Institute of American Indian Arts in Santa Fe, I traveled back and forth between New Mexico and Oklahoma, and I frequently traveled between two different accents. Once I could recognize the difference between a New Mexico accent and an Oklahoma accent, I began to hear the difference between Tahlequah and Lawton, and then between Cherokee and Kiowa. I'm not one for talking. I'm more of a listener. I'm good at one-on-one conversations. Because of this trait, I started to pick up on subtle pauses and phrases. After years of listening and contemplating, I finally had a distinctive Kiowa voice and a distinctive Cherokee voice that effectively juxtaposed these two different tribes.

Ever Geimausaddle was born out of a desire to show readers how Native families are tightly knit, and how we solidify bonds through rituals that connect extended family—our cousins are our siblings and our aunts are our mothers—so traditional kinship customs are alive and well in our communities. In a rapidly shrinking world, Natives, like everyone else, are modern constructs of a global community. And so Ever has no boundaries. He is as much Kiowa as he is Cherokee as he is Mexican. He is pulled in numerous directions and pushes back with the ferocity of his ancestors. Ever destroys walls built by metal and emotion. And isn't this the universal human condition? Our desires and identities are shaped first by those who love us the hardest, who pick up the edges of the blanket in our honor, but ultimately, by our will to make the future our own.

Questions for Discussion

1. How does Lena's quilt tie into Ever Geimausaddle's identity?

2. What are the similarities between Ever Geimausaddle and his grandfather, Vincent? How do Ever's choices propel his life in a direction different from that of his grandfather?

3. How does Vincent's last attempt to heal his grandsons relate to living with honor?

4. Why is Ever so aggressive?

5. What are the subtle and obvious ways in which toxic masculinity play out in Ever's life? And what does each narrator do to alter Ever's identity as a man?

6. What do the time jumps in the novel say about memory? What aspects of Ever's life have you as the reader inserted in lieu of the missing time?

7. Why does Sissy tell Lonnie's story?

8. How does Lonnie serve as a foil?

9. What are the similarities in how Ever, Sissy, and Turtle engage with Lonnie?

10. Why does Ever become obsessed with finding the person who broke the bench at the powwow?

11. How do honor and dishonor play out in Ever's relationship with Lonnie? How does the death of Ever's daughter change the course of his life?

12. Why does Ever rescue Leander?

13. What is the cultural significance of adoption in Plains Tribe culture?

14. Why are Lena's quilts so important to Opbee?

15. What did Opbee learn from Lena? And what does Opbee want to teach Ever?

16. What has each narrator taught Ever about family and community? To what lengths does Ever go to obtain his home?

17. How do you think each narrator would have acted differently from Ever in the final scene?

DALTON PERSE

OSCAR HOKEAH is a citizen of Cherokee Nation and the Kiowa Tribe of Oklahoma from his mother's side, and has Mexican heritage through his father. He holds an MA in English with a concentration in Native American literature from the University of Oklahoma, as well as a BFA in creative writing from the Institute of American Indian Arts (IAIA), with a minor in Indigenous Liberal Studies. He is a recipient of a Truman Capote Literary Trust scholarship through IAIA and is also a winner of the Native Writer Award through the Taos Summer Writers Conference. His short stories have been published in *South Dakota Review*, *American Short Fiction*, *Yellow Medicine Review*, *Surreal South*, and *Red Ink Journal*. He works with Indian Child Welfare in Tahlequah, Oklahoma.